Wedding Bells at Lake Como

The perfect destination for love!

Italy's picturesque Lake Como is the perfect destination for love, except the path to happy-ever-after isn't always smooth...

Cousins Gianna and Carla aren't looking for romance. Gianna's nursing a broken heart and Carla's wed to the family business. Until charismatic brothers Dario and Franco arrive on Lake Como's stunning shores...and sweep them off their feet!

Find out what happens when a case of mistaken identity leads to a fake engagement in

Bound by a Ring and a Secret

Available now!

And look out for Carla and Franco's story

Coming soon!

Dear Reader,

Does saying the same thing repeatedly make it a reality? Not necessarily. But when you put those words into action, it definitely becomes harder to tell the difference between fiction and reality.

Gianna Capillini has never had any luck in matters of the heart so she's closing herself off to love. Her spontaneous engagement has ended before it had truly begun. Now she plans to focus on her professional future, because to compound matters, she's abruptly quit her job, too. And she isn't ready to share this news with anyone—especially her beautiful, successful best friend.

Businessman Dario Marchello has a secret—he's a bestselling fiction writer. But he's got writer's block and a pressing deadline. He's come to Lake Como for the quiet to write, but when his rambunctious dog brings Gianna and Dario together, everything changes.

Though neither have an interest in a romantic relationship, they do have something in common— keeping their reason for being at the villa a secret from those closest to them. Spontaneously these two strangers become an engaged couple—all fictional, of course. But as time goes by, the lines between reality and fiction start to blur.

Happy reading,

Jennifer

Bound by a Ring and a Secret

—

Jennifer Faye

HARLEQUIN
Romance

ISBN-13: 978-1-335-56701-7

Bound by a Ring and a Secret

Copyright © 2021 by Jennifer F. Stroka

This edition published by arrangement with Harlequin Books S.A.

For questions and comments about the quality of this book,
please contact us at CustomerService@Harlequin.com.

Harlequin Enterprises ULC
22 Adelaide St. West, 40th Floor
Toronto, Ontario M5H 4E3, Canada
www.Harlequin.com

Printed in U.S.A.

Award-winning author **Jennifer Faye** pens fun, heartwarming contemporary romances with rugged cowboys, sexy billionaires and enchanting royalty. Internationally published, with books translated into nine languages, she is a two-time winner of the *RT Book Reviews* Reviewers' Choice Award. She has also won the CataRomance Reviewers' Choice Award, been named a Top Pick author and been nominated for numerous other awards.

Books by Jennifer Faye

Harlequin Romance

The Bartolini Legacy

The Prince and the Wedding Planner
The CEO, the Puppy and Me
The Italian's Unexpected Heir

Greek Island Brides

Carrying the Greek Tycoon's Baby
Claiming the Drakos Heir
Wearing the Greek Millionaire's Ring

Once Upon a Fairytale

Beauty and Her Boss
Miss White and the Seventh Heir
Fairytale Christmas with the Millionaire

Her Christmas Pregnancy Surprise

Visit the Author Profile page
at Harlequin.com for more titles.

For Lucas Lee.

Welcome to the world, sweetie!

You are a bundle of heartwarming smiles and contagious giggles.

You light up my life! Love you!

Praise for Jennifer Faye

CHAPTER ONE

HOME AGAIN.

Gianna Cappellini didn't smile.

Today, the usual euphoria of returning to the small Italian village of Gemma was lacking. Whereas her home was normally her sanctuary— a place to settle in and unwind—this time it felt different. *She* felt different.

As the hired car moved closer to her destination, she wrung her hands as she stared out the back-seat window. It was a sunny June day without a cloud in the sky. As picturesque Lake Como came into view, she merely sighed in relief.

Her gaze momentarily strayed to her still bare ring finger. Another romance had ended in disaster. Looking back, how could it have ended any other way? She'd wanted so badly to be loved that she'd tried to be someone she wasn't.

It hadn't always been that way. In the beginning, she and Naldo had rebounded into each other after messy breakups. Naldo had flirted with her and she'd fallen hard for his not-so-original lines. Things turned serious quickly as they talked about their future—him continuing to host his hit television show while she stayed in the background working the camera as she followed him around the world.

And then suddenly he dumped her. There hadn't been so much as a warning or a conversation. Just a simple, *I can't do this anymore. It's over.* And then he'd refused to speak to her. The jerk!

Her rosy glasses fell away as reality bumped hard into her. And she didn't like what she saw. She had been so busy being congenial—so agreeable—with everything he said or did that she barely recognized herself. How did she lose herself? What had happened to all the things that were important to her?

But all that was behind her now—for the most part. Tonight, she'd get to sleep in her own comfy bed. Oh, how she'd missed it. There would be no more restless nights in a tent—no more roughing it on uneven ground. She didn't even want to think about all the other luxuries she'd done without in the past several weeks.

And come tomorrow, she'd figure out what came next.

One of those things would be facing her cousin and explaining things. Thankfully, her cousin was the only person she'd confided in about her whirlwind romance and the expected engagement. And even then, she'd kept the details to the bare minimum, not even mentioning his famous name as she hadn't wanted to jinx things before the engagement was made official with a diamond ring.

Now that the relationship had imploded, what would she say to her cousin? *It was just one of those things.* Or the truth: she had the worst luck where men were concerned.

The car dropped her off at the edge of the village, allowing her to stop by the market and pick up a few essentials before heading to the villa. She hadn't been home in a little more than a month and during that time she'd used a local real-estate management service to rent out her place. She worked as a camerawoman for a nature channel and she'd come to rely on the extra funds from renting her house. It wasn't ideal but it supplemented her savings. And those savings were what would keep her afloat until her agent found her a new gig.

After picking up cream for her coffee and a few other groceries, she paid and headed for the exit. Taped to the door, she noticed a flyer for Fiorire Botanical Gardens' prestigious annual photography competition. Gianna had always wanted to enter but never had the time. The entry deadline was coming up. She tucked the information in the back of her mind.

She stepped out of the store with a sack of

groceries in one hand and her luggage in the other. It was then that she realized in her haste to complete her errands she'd sent the car away and would now have to walk the rest of the way home. Not that it was far—perhaps a fifteen-minute walk, give or take a couple of minutes, depending on how fast she moved. But part of her travel was uphill on a bumpy dirt road. There were only a handful of villas on the dead-end road where she lived. Hers was the last one—

"Gianna?" came a distant voice.

She didn't have to turn around to know who was calling her name. It was her cousin—the one person she'd really hoped to avoid. It wasn't that she didn't love her cousin. In truth, she loved Carla dearly. She was more like a sister than a cousin. But Gianna just wasn't ready to admit that she'd failed at romance. Again.

Pretending she hadn't heard her cousin, she kept moving in the opposite direction. Her steps were sure and quick. She forced herself to hold her head high though the guilt of her actions weighed on her.

She told herself she just needed a little time to settle in and get her bearings. Once she found the right words and was able to say them without feeling like an utter failure, she'd be able to face her rich, beautiful and successful cousin, who had her life totally together, including her pick of successful men. Why couldn't she be more like her? More congenial? More beautiful? More whatever it was that made every man that met Carla immediately fall in love with her?

But none of that mattered anymore. Gianna was done with men. She'd lost herself in one too many relationships—dismissing what was important to her to make them happy—and she wasn't going to let that happen again.

Outside of the village, Gianna lowered her head. She promised herself that she'd make this up to her cousin. With her gaze focused on the ruts that constituted a road, she continued trudging down the desolate lane that was surrounded by lush vegetation and trees. The suitcase's little wheels rolled over the gravel, making a terrible racket. When a wheel got stuck, which happened repeatedly, she gave it a forceful yank.

At the end of the lane was her home; the stately pale pink villa with white trim and a terracotta roof that she'd inherited from her grandmother. Its beauty was timeless. It sat upon a hillside, providing a stunning view of Lake Como.

And what the villa lacked in modern style, it made up for with rustic charm. With seven bedrooms and five bathrooms, it was far too large for one person. And yet Gianna couldn't imagine parting with it. Just like her grandmother, she loved it here.

Woof. Woof.

A medium-sized dog with short light tan fur

emerged from the bushes. It rushed into the lane, blocking her.

It stopped.

Gianna stopped. Now what?

Her grip on her luggage handle tightened. Her body tensed. She stared at the dog. He stared back at her. Then, drawing on the knowledge of animals she'd gained from working on nature documentaries, she averted her gaze ever so slightly. She didn't want the dog to misinterpret her staring at him as a sign of aggression.

She searched her memory and was certain she'd never seen this dog before. She wasn't sure if he was friendly or not. But they couldn't just stand here trying not to stare at each other.

"Hi, boy." She forced a smile.

His tail swished back and forth. That was a good sign.

The dog approached her. Gianna wasn't sure what she should do, so she did nothing. Her heart continued to pound. As he drew nearer, her palms grew moist. He could probably sense her nervousness from a mile away. And yet his tail kept wagging as he grew closer.

And then he stopped in front of her. He sat down and gazed up at her. It was then that she noticed he had the kindest big brown eyes. She held out her hand to him and his dark nose sniffed it. She proceeded to run her hand over his head. He rubbed against her hand before dancing around in a circle.

It appeared they'd become fast friends. She breathed a sigh of relief. He might be rather big in size but she sensed by his bright eyes and his playful behavior that he wasn't very old.

"Hi, buddy. What are you doing out here?" And then she realized how silly it was asking a dog a question. It wasn't like he could answer her. But it seemed wrong not to speak to him, like she was ignoring him or something. "Do you have a collar?"

She knelt down and continued petting him. There was a depression in his fur as though he normally wore a collar, but there wasn't one there now. Strange.

It was obvious he had a home—a home where he was cared for. His fur was clean and groomed. He was well fed. And he had manners. So that told her somewhere in this world, someone was searching for their four-footed friend. And most likely beside themselves with worry.

She slowly moved her hand to her pocket and then withdrew her phone. She didn't want to make any sudden movements and startle the dog.

Her phone flashed that the battery was low. Hopefully, it'd hold out long enough to take a couple photos.

"I'm just going to take your picture. Hold still."

He did everything but stay still. He sniffed her

and then the camera. About the fifth try, she finally had a usable photo that she could post on social media in an attempt to find his human.

Gianna's gaze met the dog's. "Don't worry. We'll get you home. In the meantime, would you like to come home with me?"

She grabbed the handle on her suitcase and then looked at him. "Come on. We'll go to my place and I'll make a few phone calls. We'll get you home in no time."

She started walking because what else was she going to do? He was too big for her to carry. She really hoped he'd follow her. She didn't like the thought of leaving him out here on his own. In a way, she felt responsible for him. She didn't want anything to happen to him.

When she turned back, she found the dog was still sitting in the same spot. This wasn't her problem, she told herself. She should just keep going. The dog probably knew his way home. But then she recalled his missing collar. What did it mean? Had someone dumped him on the side of the road? The thought made her heart sink down to her cute white sandals.

"I have food," she said, hoping he would understand what she was saying. "Food. Are you hungry?"

He cocked his head to the side.

"Come on, boy. I'll feed you."

He got up and strolled over to her. She smiled.

Apparently, he liked to eat. Thank goodness food was a universal language. They walked side by side for a bit. Then he ran ahead and she worried he'd run away.

"Puppy! Puppy, come back."

He rounded the corner. With the heavy green vegetation, she wasn't able to see where he'd gone. She tried to run after him, but her luggage got hung up in a rut. She had to stop and free it. By then she knew the dog would be long gone. She just hoped nothing happened to him.

When her home finally came into sight, she sighed. She was beginning to feel like her journey would never end. But at last she was here. She opened the gate and let herself onto the grounds. It was here that she could lick her wounds while figuring out a new plan for her life because aside from losing her almost-fiancé, she'd also quit her job. She had a lot to figure out.

It wasn't until she reached the door that she noticed the dog sitting off to the side. How did he get past the gate? She let go of her luggage and turned to the dog. "How did you know I lived here? Are you psychic or something?"

Woof. Woof-woof.

"Well, I'm not quite sure what you're trying to tell me because I don't speak dog. But since you're here, how about you come inside? I'll see what I can find for you to eat."

She unlocked the door and followed him in. A

cursory glance around the spacious living room and then the large modern kitchen told her things were in their appropriate place. She had to admit that renting out her house made her uncomfortable, even if the money was quite good. She loved this place. It held some of her most treasured childhood memories. And she'd be heartbroken if anything ever happened to it.

Woof.

She smiled as she glanced at the dog, who was now sitting by her side as though they'd been together for years. He looked up at her with such warmth in his big brown eyes. What had she done to deserve his trust? And yet here he was sitting next to her, waiting for the food she'd promised him.

She moved to her luggage and the cloth shopping bag she'd draped around the handle. Inside, she had some fresh baked bread, meats and cheeses. Quite honestly, she wasn't sure what dogs were allowed to eat but she couldn't imagine that in a pinch a sandwich would be totally frowned upon. And so that's what she did. She made her new friend a sandwich and one for herself. Her stomach rumbled in anticipation. She hadn't eaten yet that day. She'd been getting by on caffeine, but her stomach was in utter rebellion over its liquid diet.

She was quite tempted to take a bite of her sandwich first, but when she glanced over at those needy eyes, she couldn't resist him. This pup had such a sweet gentle soul.

"Here you go." She held out a quarter of the sandwich.

The dog carefully took it without so much as nipping her. He chewed…and chewed…and chewed…and finally swallowed. She'd been worried he wouldn't like the sandwich, but as he looked at her for more, she realized he'd liked it just fine. She took a bite of her own sandwich. Not bad. The dog started impatiently nudging her elbow with his cold wet nose.

"Okay. Okay. I'm getting it." As she picked up the plate with his sandwich, she said, "You know, now that you're eating me out of house and home, I'll have to go back to the store." She held out the next piece. "Here you go—"

"Hey! What are you doing?"

The boom of the unfamiliar male voice made her jump. The plate slipped from her hand. It crashed to the floor. Little pieces of glass pelted her ankles and feet.

What in the world? Her heart leaped into her throat. She sensed someone standing behind her. What was she to do now?

CHAPTER TWO

THE POUNDING OF her heart echoed in her ears.

An intruder in these parts was quite unheard of. In the village of Gemma, everyone knew your name. That was one of the many charms that convinced Gianna to keep her grandmother's villa. But this man's deep voice was unfamiliar to her. Who was he? And what was he doing in her house?

Gianna had to do something to defend herself. She visually searched for a weapon, finding one on the stove. Her fingers wrapped around the handle of a heavy cast-iron skillet. It could definitely do some damage.

Swinging the pan up over her head, she turned. "You better leave. Now."

The man's dark eyes widened. His gaze moved upward to the heavy pan in her hands. He stood his ground. Then his gaze returned to meet hers.

"I'm not going anywhere."

She didn't know whether to be afraid of him or utterly frustrated. "Then I'm ringing the *polizia*."

"You do realize you'll have to put down the pan before you can phone anyone?" His eyes twinkled with amusement.

She glared at him. This wasn't funny. He was supposed to be intimidated. Not amused.

"Leave. Now." She mustered up her most intimidating voice and gestured toward the door with her head because the pan was too heavy to hold with just one hand.

The man crossed his arms, making his biceps bulge. He didn't so much as budge a millimeter.

He was strikingly tall as she had to crane her neck to stare into his eyes. His brown hair was a bit longer on top with a little curl. It was a casual look to go with the scruff along his prominent jawline.

A navy T-shirt fit snug across his broad, strong shoulders and clung to his muscular chest. She swallowed hard. She shouldn't be checking him out. Whether he was hot or not, he'd broken into her home.

His phone buzzed. He withdrew it from his pocket, checked the screen and then slipped it back in his pocket.

When her gaze once more met his, there was amusement dancing in his eyes. He'd caught her giving him a brief once-over. She inwardly groaned. That was not good—not good at all.

Still, she couldn't deny that he was quite handsome in that playboy sort of way. Not that she was interested. First, he was an intruder in her house. Second, he was infuriating in the way he didn't take her seriously. And lastly, she was done with men, cute or otherwise.

In an effort to reach for her phone, she tried releasing the pan's handle with one hand, but the weight of the cast iron was too much to hold with just one hand. Maybe she should have spent more time at the gym and less time traipsing around the continent with a sweet-talking man who didn't really care about her and was just biding his time until his ex stepped back into his life.

"I have a dog," she said, glancing down at the stray pup. It was hidden from the man's view by the kitchen island.

The man smiled. "You mean *my* dog?"

His dog?

The man stepped forward. "Tito. Here, boy." Immediately, the dog darted around the kitchen island. The man knelt down to pet the dog. "What are you doing letting a stranger in our house—"

"Your house?"

The man continued talking to the dog as though he hadn't heard her. "You're supposed to protect the place. Instead, you run off. I've been looking everywhere for you."

The dog whined and then laid down in front of the man. The pup lowered his head to the kitchen floor and then covered his muzzle with his paw.

Inwardly, Gianna was going, *Aww...* But outwardly she wasn't letting down her guard with this man. He had a lot of explaining to do. Like why he'd walked into her house like he owned it.

The man straightened and turned to her. "If you put down the pan, we can discuss the fact that you're in my house."

Her arms slowly lowered, not because she trusted the man, but rather from muscle fatigue. She studied the man's strikingly handsome face, looking for amusement, as though he were making a joke. But the look he gave her was very serious. How could he believe he had any rights to this place? This house had been in her family for generations.

She placed the pan on the countertop. Gianna picked up her phone, finding the battery had finally died. But he didn't have to know that. She held it in her hand as though she were ready to make a call. "Okay. Explain yourself."

His eyes twinkled again as though he found everything about her amusing. Well, the feeling didn't go both ways.

"My name is Dario Marchello."

Why does that name sound familiar? She instinctively knew she should know his name, but she just couldn't place it. The jet lag was causing her mind to be foggy.

"Well, Mr. Marchello, you still haven't said what you're doing here?"

"Call me, Dario. And I've rented the place last month and this month."

Her mouth gaped. That's how she knew the name. He was her renter. A sexy renter at that, but he still had to go.

"And who would you be?"

"Gianna Cappellini. I own this house."

Dario glanced around as though he were looking for someone else. "And you live in this big house all by yourself?"

"Yes, I do," she said proudly. It wasn't until the words were spoken that she realized she was speaking to a stranger. She rushed to add, "But I have family in the area." It was true. "My cousin is on her way here." Sort of true. "She'll be over anytime now." A bit of a stretch. But knowing her cousin, she was sure to visit sooner rather than later. Then, turning the conversation back on him, she asked, "And you rented such a big house just for yourself?"

He nodded. "And Tito."

Enough with the war of words. She had things to do. She glanced down at the tiny pieces of shattered plate all over the floor. "I need to clean this mess up before someone gets hurt."

"I'll help you," he offered.

"Why would you do that?"

"Because I startled you, causing you to drop the plate. For that, I'm sorry."

She was impressed with his manners. For

the next several minutes, they worked together, cleaning up the shards while keeping the dog away.

When his phone buzzed again, she said, "If you need to take that—"

"It can wait." His tone was a bit terse, as though he was intent on avoiding whoever was on the other end of that phone call.

Once everything was in order, she turned to him. "Thank you for the help, but I still don't understand what you're doing here."

His dark brows rose. "You're the one that isn't supposed to be here."

And this is where things became rather sticky. "I don't think you understand. Our agreement was for a one-month rental."

"And then I spoke with the property management company to see if it was available for another month. They said it was."

Gianna inwardly groaned. She recalled the management company trying to reach her numerous times, but at the time she'd been in a remote area of France where cell signals were hit or miss. There was one call where words were broken by stretches of silence. Gianna knew they had a question about the house but after repeated tries, she couldn't make out what they were saying. She trusted them, as the company's owner was friends with her extended family, and so she'd said to use their best judgment. Perhaps she shouldn't have been that trusting.

"They were mistaken," she said.

"I have it in writing. And I've already paid."

Hmm...that explained the mysterious increase in her bank account. This was getting complicated. She wanted to offer him money to just go away and leave her alone in her misery but her savings were greatly needed now that she was jobless.

It's not that she'd been planning to quit her job—at least not so suddenly—but rather it became necessary. After all, how do you continue to work with the man you thought you had a future with when he suddenly dumps you for his ex? It was beyond her powers of diplomacy. Space—lots of space—was the only solution. And quite frankly, the allure of sleeping under the stars and being one with nature had long since passed her by.

"I'm sorry for the mix-up," she said. "But I'll give you back the money you paid for the extra month."

Frown lines marred his much too handsome face. "This isn't about the money."

"What's it about, then?"

A muscle in his clean-shaven cheek twitched as he pressed his hands to his lean waist. "I went through the proper process to rent this house for another month. I paid the fee and have the paperwork. I don't see why I should leave."

"But surely there has to be somewhere else for you to go."

He shook his head. "This place is exactly what I need right now. Besides, everything in the area is rented. It's the summer. Families want to get away from the hustle and bustle of the city. And quite frankly, I don't have the time to search for other accommodations when I've already secured this place until the end of the month."

There had to be some sort of compromise. But what?

And so she mentally scrambled for a way to get this man out of her life. If money wasn't going to work, then she'd have to give him what he wanted.

She lifted her gaze to meet his. "Fine. If I can find you similar accommodations nearby, will you move out?"

His phone buzzed again. His dark brows drew together as he checked the caller ID. "I better get this. Excuse me."

She nodded in understanding, even if she was anxious to come to some sort of understanding with him. There was no way he was staying here—with her. Even if there was plenty of room.

Dario had stepped outside to the patio area. He left the door ajar and though she wasn't trying to eavesdrop, as his voice rose in volume, it carried into the kitchen.

She could excuse herself to another part of the house, but this was her home. And he was an unwanted, unwelcome guest. She stood her ground.

"Yes. I got your notes."

A moment of silence passed. "No, I don't know when I'll get back to you. I need some time."

More silence. "Two weeks is impossible. What about six weeks?"

She sure was curious what all the negotiating was about. She sat down on a kitchen stool as she watched Dario pace back and forth along the length of the pool with his dog right behind him.

He raked his fingers through his hair. "Fine. I'll have it back to you by the end of the month." He ended the call.

Gianna turned back to the counter as though she were contemplating eating more of her sandwich, but with her stomach twisted in a knot, it was impossible to eat.

"Everything okay?" The words slipped past her lips before she remembered they weren't friends—not even close.

"It's fine." His tone let her know it was anything but fine. "What were we talking about?"

She really wanted to ask him about the phone conversation that had left him utterly distracted, but as it was none of her business, she let it go.

"We were talking about me finding you alternative accommodations."

"Right." He hesitated. "I suppose that would work, but I'd have to approve it first."

The distraction had helped her. At last, she could take a full breath. "Good." A slight smile of triumph pulled at the corners of her lips. "I'll get to work on it. I'll let you know what I find."

"Don't get too excited. There's nothing available. I already looked before I knew this place was available for another month."

The slight lift of the corners of her mouth suddenly dipped into a frown. "Maybe you missed something."

"Maybe." But he didn't sound convinced. "I'll just move my things from the master bedroom to the guesthouse before I go check the fence to see how Tito escaped."

"Oh. Okay." She didn't know how she felt about sharing her place with a total stranger. But at least the guesthouse was completely separate from the main house. A large in-ground pool and patio area separated the two accommodations.

Without another word, he set off toward the master bedroom—her bedroom. He'd been sleeping in her bed. Delicious visions of him in nothing but his boxers slipping between her sheets were suddenly all she could see, and the house started to feel uncomfortably warm.

She stepped outside, hoping a breeze would cool her down. There had to be another place for him to stay because no way were they spending the month together. Not a chance.

CHAPTER THREE

THIS DEVELOPMENT WAS most unwelcome.

Dario Marchello had no desire to share his idyllic getaway. Still, if he had to share it, Gianna was certainly a beautiful housemate. As soon as the thought came to him, he dismissed it. His entire future was on the line. He didn't have time to be distracted.

Nor did he indulge in relationships that lasted more than two weeks. He'd learned that any longer than this and the women he dated started to think of their relationship as a committed one. And nothing could be further from the truth.

It was stamped into his DNA that committed relationships don't work. His parents' marriage ended in divorce when he was young. Not only did they give up on each other, but they'd also given up on him and his brother.

His jaw clenched tight as he recalled being dumped on his paternal grandparents as though he and his brother were pets that just didn't work out. He tried not to think about the past. Happy memories were few and far between. It was best to focus on the future.

He made short work of transferring his things to the guesthouse. After which he went in search of Tito's escape path before his beloved dog pulled another disappearing act. It didn't take long to find the hole under the fence and Tito's missing collar. Dario filled in the hole, topping it with some large rocks to deter a repeat performance.

His thoughts drifted back to Gianna and why she was living in this great big villa all alone. What was her story?

The writer in him started crafting different backstories for her, from an orphaned heiress to a young widow. When he realized he was still thinking about Gianna instead of focusing on this agent's notes, he chased images of the mystery woman from his mind.

A couple of hours later, he was still sitting in the patio area, staring at his agent's comments on his laptop. He read them over and over as though they'd suddenly enlighten him as to what to write next. So far it hadn't worked.

When he heard Gianna moving about in the large kitchen, he glanced at his Rolex. It was dinnertime. He should probably do something about that, but first he wanted to write a few words, any words. Otherwise, his entire day would be a waste and that was unacceptable.

He stared at the blinking cursor. He shifted in his chair, not finding a comfortable position. Wondering if anything urgent was needed at the family business, he flipped to his email. Nothing new. What did he expect? He was, after all, on vacation, using the unused days he'd been accruing since joining his grandfather and older brother at Marchello Spices.

He switched the screen back to his manuscript. He once more stared at the blinking cursor. With an exasperated sigh, he closed the laptop and set it aside. He got to his feet and moved toward the kitchen. He rapped his knuckles on the framework of the open French doors. Tito was right beside him.

Gianna jumped. She spun around from where she was peering into the fridge. "You startled me."

Dario cleared his throat. "Sorry. I seem to have a habit of doing that."

Tito rushed over to her. It appeared she'd already won over his dog. She fussed over him and Tito ate it up.

"Thankfully, I didn't have anything in my hands this time." She sent him a tentative smile that didn't quite reach her eyes. "What do you need?"

Need? Well, that would be something she couldn't give him—more time and the right words to fix his novel. Sooner or later, his older brother would insist he get back to the office. And he couldn't blame him. They weren't raised to sit back and do nothing—even if they were fortunate enough to come from great wealth.

He shook his head. "Nothing."

Her pretty eyes clouded with confusion. "Then what are you doing in here?"

"Oh. Right." What was wrong with him? He wasn't normally stumbling over his words. After all, words were his thing. At least he thought they were, but these revisions were proving otherwise. He swallowed hard. "I was just going to see if I could take you to dinner." When her fine brows rose in surprise and then settled into a line of suspicion, he added, "I meant as a thank-you, you know, for letting me stay here."

"But I didn't say you could stay."

"Oh. Does that mean you found an available rental?" Disappointment assailed him as he'd gotten quite used to this place. There was a peacefulness here that he'd never felt before. And the view of the lake was relaxing—maybe too relaxing.

"Actually, that was something I needed to discuss with you. I, um, called around and there's nothing available."

He struggled not to send her an I-told-you-so smile. And then before she could tell him that he had to move out immediately, he blurted, "I don't mind staying in the guesthouse."

"I don't know."

"Listen, your rental agency ran a background check on me before renting the house to me. I've already paid for the month in advance. And quite honestly, I'm a great tenant. I'm so quiet you won't even know I'm here."

She didn't say anything, as though taking in everything he'd just said. With each blink of her eyes, it was like she was processing the information he'd given her.

"What is it you're doing here?" she asked.

His immediate response was to give her some flimsy excuse, but he had no reason to hide his actions from her. She was a perfect stranger—someone he'd never see again. "I'm writing a book."

He waited for her shocked response, but she appeared to take his answer in stride—something his family wouldn't do. His grandfather would be horrified to know he preferred writing to working in the family business. His brother would undoubtedly be disappointed. And his grandmother, well, he wasn't sure what her reaction would be.

"That's interesting."

"And this place gives me the privacy I need to finish the book." He couldn't tell if he was swaying her into letting him stay or not.

She seemed to mull over his words. "And you'd be all right in the guesthouse?"

It wasn't as comfy as the main house but it would do. And best of all, his family didn't know where to find him. If he were back at his Verona apartment, his brother would stop by regularly, wondering what he was up to on his time off. His grandfather, who still had one foot in the company, would find excuses for him to come to the office. And his grandmother would expect him for the usual Sunday dinner. But here at the lake, he didn't have to live up to anyone's expectations.

Gianna's rosy lips pursed together as though she were giving the situation serious thought. "Perhaps we could give it a trial period. Say, until the end of the week."

"But that's only two days away."

"Exactly." She smiled as though she'd solved both of their problems.

Did she really think she'd find cause to eject him that easily? She didn't know him very well. He would win her over. One way or the other. Because he wasn't going back to the city until he finished this book.

"Now about dinner," he said.

"No." She shook her head. "Thank you."

That was the absolute fastest rejection he'd ever received. His ego took a definite hit. And he just couldn't let it go. He had to know what she found so objectionable about him. Was it because he was now her roommate—sort of? Or did she have a boyfriend?

He ignored the sense of disappointment. She most likely had a significant other in her life. After all, she was really cute. And her beauty didn't come from a makeup kit. Hers was all natural, from her blue eyes to her long dark lashes to her pert nose and pouty lips.

With each passing moment, his curiosity grew. "May I ask why?"

"I… I don't want to go into the village."

Relief flooded his system. This too he ignored. "Are you worried your boyfriend will see you with another man?"

"Hardly. He dumped me." Her voice rose with emotion. "That lying, scheming jerk. I don't know why I ever trusted him. I should have known he wasn't over his ex when her name came up frequently. Of course, he said she was in the past, but all along I had this feeling there was more to it. But did I listen to my little voice? Nope. I shoved aside my suspicions and told myself I was being paranoid." She grabbed a pan and placed it on the stove with a loud clang. "I'm the worst judge of men. You know he isn't the first man I almost married. The first time around, I was just out of school. We'd dated for years. I had the ring and the dress. Right before I was to walk down the aisle, he bailed. If I pick them, you can bet your last dollar it won't work out."

Dario stood quietly, trying to keep his mouth from dropping open. First, what guy would dump her? It went beyond her striking face or curvy figure. He didn't know her well, but he'd observed her sharing her lunch with his dog. Only someone with a kind heart would do that. And so far she hadn't ordered him to leave. That said a lot about her.

"I'm sorry." He didn't know what else to say.

She whipped around and stared at him as though she'd forgotten he was still standing there. "You have nothing to be sorry about, but my ex does. He cost me not only a relationship but also my job and now I have to face my cousin and tell her I'm not getting married. Again."

"You were engaged?"

"Well, no. Not exactly. He mentioned it—looking back it had been way too casual—but I was in love with the idea of being in love. I wanted—no, I needed—this relationship to be the right one. And so I told my cousin. I had to tell someone or I would have burst."

He tried to piece together what he'd learned. "So what you're saying is that you don't want to go into the village because you're avoiding your cousin, who thinks you're happily engaged. And you're not ready to tell her how things ended?"

Her gaze met his. "Exactly."

"Isn't she going to figure it out?"

She shrugged. "I suppose. But if it's later, it won't be the shortest engagement in the history of man."

"I bet there's been shorter." Her narrowed gaze let him know he wasn't helping the situation. "Okay. We'll eat in." His gaze moved to the stove where there were now four empty pans. "It looks like you already have something in mind."

Her gaze moved to the stove before turning back to him. Color filled her cheeks. "I don't know why I did that. I don't cook."

"Oh."

She was full of surprises. He had the feeling living with her for the next month definitely wasn't going to be boring. Far from it. But if he wanted to finish his book, he was going to need to keep his distance because she was a distraction—a beautiful one—but a distraction nonetheless.

"How about I cook?" he suggested. "You know, as a thank-you for letting me stay. I was planning to make spaghetti Bolognese. How does that sound to you?"

"Anything I don't burn sounds good to me." She turned to put the pans away. "I'm sorry."

"For what?"

"I can't believe I dumped all that on you. It wasn't fair. It's just that I've been keeping it all inside for the past two weeks until we finished shooting the segment and now that I'm home, well, I just can't bear to face my cousin. She'll look at me like I'm pathetic. At this point, it would do me in."

"So you told a stranger. No big deal. I won't tell anyone so long as you don't tell anyone that I'm here writing a book."

"You've got yourself a deal."

"Should we shake on it?" It seemed like the natural thing to do.

But when his hand engulfed hers, the jolt of attraction that zinged through his body was not natural. It was extraordinary. He wondered if she could feel it too. What would she say if he were to seal this deal with a kiss? His gaze lingered on her pouty lips. Would she swoon in his arms? The thought definitely appealed to him—

She jerked her hand away. The moment was lost. Was it possible she'd read his mind? Impossible. He couldn't even believe he was having those thoughts about her after he got done reminding himself how important it was for him not to get distracted until his book was submitted.

Her cheeks darkened with color. "I… I should get out of your way." She turned her back to him and then turned around again. "Unless you need my help?"

"I've got it. Thanks."

He set to work and realized Tito was missing. Usually the dog followed him everywhere. He glanced out at the patio and immediately spotted Tito. As if by magnetic attraction, the pup clung to Gianna's side. She knelt down and hugged him. If Dario didn't know better, he'd think she'd stolen his dog.

But it wasn't Tito he was worried about. It was himself. He'd have to keep his distance from Gianna. He didn't think straight when he was around her.

CHAPTER FOUR

WHAT HAD GOTTEN into her?

The following morning, Gianna made herself comfortable on the patio. She was still berating herself. Since when did she tell a total stranger about her personal life? Apparently, starting now. Gianna could still remember the way Dario had looked at her. He must think she'd totally lost her mind. And she couldn't blame him.

At least dinner had gone better. The spaghetti had been cooked to perfection. Not too soft and not too chewy. And the sauce had the perfect balance of spices. If he weren't a writer, she'd suggest he become a chef.

Though she didn't say it because he had been very quiet throughout dinner. As such, she'd done the same. She'd already said more than enough for one day. And after dinner, she'd insisted on cleaning up—alone. It was the least she could do.

Today, her first order of business was calling her agent. As much as she enjoyed being home, she couldn't afford not to work.

The conversation thankfully didn't last long because she didn't want to dwell on why she'd quit her last job. The bad news was that there were no film crew jobs available, but he'd let her know when something opened up.

In the meantime, she needed to get it all together before she saw her cousin. She needed to figure out what to say without breaking down in tears. Because every time she thought of what a fool she'd been, the tears of frustration welled up in her eyes. When would she learn not to be so trusting—

"Good morning." Speaking of being trusting, her unexpected houseguest strolled out to the patio. It was then that she noticed his tousled hair. It looked as though he had run his fingers through it many times that morning.

"Morning? But it's almost lunchtime."

His brows rose. "Is it that late already?"

"It is."

"I guess I got caught up in my work and lost track of time."

"There's coffee in the kitchen if you want some."

"Thanks. That sounds good. I ran out a bit ago and didn't take the time to make more." He paused next to Tito and bent down to scratch behind his ears. "I wondered where you'd gotten off to."

"He came begging for some of my eggs and toast."

"Sorry about that. He is a bit of a beggar."

"With those puppy eyes, it's impossible to say no."

Once Dario had a cup full of coffee, he returned to the patio. He stopped next to a chair at the table. "Mind if I join you?"

"Not at all." She closed her laptop.

"I didn't mean to interrupt your work."

She shook her head. "Trust me. You weren't."

"Are you sure, because I can go back to my room—"

"No. Stay. I wasn't working. Remember? I quit my job."

"Oh, that's right. Sorry. You know it's probably not too late to get it back. Just tell them you quit in the heat of the moment and now you regret it. What is it you do?"

"I'm a camerawoman. I've been working on a nature series." And then she realized the conversation had drifted back to her and her problems. Not a subject she wanted to discuss. "But enough about me. What's it like to write a book?"

He shook his head. "You don't want to hear about that."

"Oh, but I do. I have to admit, I'm quite curious."

"Well, the majority of the time, I'm staring at

the wall, hoping for a bit of inspiration to come to me."

"And the rest of the time?"

"I'm typing."

"Typing?" He certainly wasn't one for spilling details without a lot of encouragement. "What are you typing? Your life story?"

"Close." He smiled. "Just joking. I write fiction. Or rather, I've written the book and now I'm going back and fixing it."

"Wow. And that's what you've been doing here for the past month?" When he nodded, she said, "That's very impressive."

"Really?"

"Why do you sound surprised?"

"Because my family would think it's a cute hobby but not practical. They want me to have what they deem a *real job*."

"I'm sorry. I understand. I'm not doing what my family thinks I should be doing either."

"And what's that?"

"Getting married. Having my husband work at the family market so he can one day take over. And let's not forget the grandkids. Not that those aren't great things but I need to figure out what makes me happy before I can make someone else happy."

His gaze searched hers. "And did you do that? Do you know what makes you happy?"

She shrugged. "I thought I did. I loved standing behind a camera and then later editing the scenes."

"And now?"

She shrugged. "I still like being behind a camera but I don't know about the rest. Maybe I've just been on the road for too long, living out of hotels and tents."

"Tents?"

She smiled and nodded. "That surprises you?"

"No." He smiled. "Okay. Yes, it does. I don't know any women who would sleep outside in a tent."

"We roughed it for a lot of the footage. Our meals were heated on a portable grill and we won't even discuss the bathroom and shower arrangements." She shook her head. Though some of her experiences were absolutely amazing, there were other parts she just didn't want to recall.

"And your ex—he was part of the crew?"

"No. Naldo is the host of the documentary."

"Oh. I see."

"So there's no way I can go back to that group, even if I wanted to. And I don't want to—"

"Gianna?" a familiar voice called from a distance.

It was her cousin, Carla. Panic launched Gianna's heart into her throat.

Gianna's first instinct was to hide inside and pretend like she wasn't home. It would be so much easier. But she'd never been one to hide. So she would face her cousin, even though she dreaded the pity that she would inevitably see in Carla's eyes when she heard about Gianna's latest romantic debacle.

And worse yet, Carla would do what Carla always did. She'd try to fix things. She would host parties—parties with lots of single men. There would be guys that were friends with Carla, there would be brothers of friends and every other eligible bachelor she could track down and invite to one of her spectacular events.

But that wasn't for Gianna. She had done the rich bachelor before. It never worked out. If she ever let herself get involved again, it would be with a man who led a simpler life. Her gaze moved across the table to her housemate. It would be someone like Dario.

Not that she was interested in him or anything. In fact, she was shocked that such a thought had crossed her mind. Her focus right now was to be on herself and what comes next in her life—not on a really sexy tempting man.

Carla stepped into the patio area with a big bright smile on her face. "There you are."

Gianna got to her feet and stepped toward her cousin. Carla approached her and wrapped her in a big warm hug. Gianna reciprocated. And then they gave each other a feathery cheek kiss as they always did when they hadn't seen each other in a while.

Gianna pulled back. "Carla, what are you doing here?"

"Well, I thought I saw you in the village yesterday. I called out to you but you must not have heard me. Anyway, I didn't have time to go after you because I was late for an appointment." Carla lifted her big dark sunglasses and rested them on her head like a hair band as she sent Gianna a bright sunny smile. "And by the time I got home, it was late. I figured you'd be tired after traveling, so I didn't bother you. So here I am now."

"Sorry. I should have called you when I got home but, as you suspected, I had jet lag."

"Where were you this time?"

"France."

Carla's eyes widened. "You do live a very exciting life."

"It's not that exciting." Far from it.

"Oh, but it is. I should go with you sometime."

"I keep telling you that you won't like roughing it in a tent and at times going without a shower or proper bathroom."

Carla's face scrunched up. "That would be unbearable. But I'd still liked to see those beautiful locations you film in person…maybe just for a day trip."

"We'll see." They'd had this conversation

many times over the last few years. It never went further than talking.

Carla moved to the side and smiled at Dario. "Hi. I'm Carla Falco, Gianna's cousin."

Dario's eyes momentarily widened. "As in Falco's Fresco Ristorante?"

Carla's smile drooped a bit. "Yes."

Dario got to his feet and stepped around the table. He extended his hand to Carla. "Nice to meet you," he said, like a true gentleman. "I'm Dario Marchello."

Carla took his hand in both of hers as her smile brightened. "It's so nice to finally meet you—"

"Excuse me." An unfamiliar male voice caused all heads to turn. "Dario, you're a hard man to find."

Carla let go of Dario's hand as they all turned at once to their visitor. A tall man approached them. Gianna noticed how her cousin's eyes lit up as she stared at their visitor. Gianna couldn't blame her. This man was definitely good-looking but not quite as handsome as Dario.

The man's gaze moved to Gianna and then paused on her cousin. "Excuse me, ladies. I'm sorry to interrupt."

"Oh, you aren't interrupting." Carla approached him. "I already did that."

The man's smile broadened, showing the dimples in his cheeks, but Gianna noticed that the smile didn't quite reach his dark eyes. The man was not happy about something, but he was working very hard to cover it up. What was up with that?

"I didn't know there was a party." The man's pointed gaze moved to Dario.

Dario crossed his arms, never once flinching from the man's lethal stare. "If there was a party, you wouldn't have been invited as you don't believe in having a good time."

The man's face remained emotionless. "I don't believe in partying when there's work to be done."

Dario stood. "So you came here to monitor my actions?"

"Do I need to?"

Wow! The tension between the two men was positively palpable. Though the stranger had dark hair and was slightly taller than Dario, their similar facial features gave away that they were brothers. Though something told her that their close biological link didn't make either of them happy at the moment.

Hoping to break the tension, Gianna stepped forward and extended her hand. "Welcome. I'm Gianna."

He gave her hand a firm shake. "I'm Franco. Dario's older brother."

Carla stepped forward. "Are you Franco Marchello, as in Marchello Spices?"

He let go of Gianna's hand and then turned to

her cousin. "I am." He studied Carla's face for a moment. "Have we met?"

"No. I've just seen your name on some of my father's business correspondence."

"I'm afraid you have the advantage. Who's your father?"

"Carlo Falco."

"Interesting. So if I wanted to talk business—"

"You'd have to speak to my father." Carla's tone held a note of bitterness.

"You two look a lot alike," Gianna said, hoping to change the subject. She knew her cousin was thoroughly annoyed with her father and his archaic thoughts about women in the business world.

"But we don't act alike," Dario said. "How did you find me?"

"It wasn't hard. You're driving a company car, remember? Those are all outfitted with GPS."

Gianna swung around to look at Dario. His lips were pressed together in a formidable line as a muscle in his cheek twitched. She frowned at him, hoping he would lighten up. She wondered if things were always this contentious between these two or if something specific had happened to cause the rift.

"It's so nice to have you here." Carla kept her attention focused on Franco. "Are you staying in the area?"

"Only for the night. I came to talk some sense

into my brother." Franco's attention moved to his brother. "What are you doing all the way out here?"

"Don't you know?" Carla asked before she leaned closer to Franco to loudly whisper, "They're engaged."

Gianna's mouth gaped. She looked at Dario, wanting him to know that she had nothing to do with her cousin jumping to such a wild conclusion.

Franco's dark brows drew together as his mouth lowered into a frown. "That's not true."

"But it is," Carla insisted. "I think it was supposed to be a secret until they make a big announcement, but since you're family, I'd have thought for sure your brother would have told you."

"You must be mistaken," Franco said to Carla as his pointed stare met Dario's. "My brother has no intention of getting married."

Carla grinned. "I think Gianna changed his mind."

Dario moved to Gianna's side. He slipped an arm around her waist and pulled her against him. And for just a fraction of a second, she liked being so close to him. It was as if they fit together. In the next heartbeat, reality came crashing in on her.

What in the world? Dario is playing along with this? Has he lost his mind?

"Dario, what are you doing?" she whispered.

Dario's gaze met hers. It was impossible to read his thoughts. "There's no sense hiding it. They were bound to learn about the engagement sooner or later."

Her mouth opened to deny such an engagement existed but Franco beat her to the punch. "So it's true?"

Dario nodded. And then he smiled, much like a Cheshire cat. "It is. Gianna and I are to be married."

"Married?" Franco sent him a skeptical look. "That's rather unexpected." His gaze moved between the two of them. "How long have you known each other?"

What was Dario doing? Heat swirled in Gianna's chest and then rushed up her neck, setting her cheeks aflame. This couldn't be happening. Dario was taking her painful experience of being dumped by her ex for his former girlfriend and using it…for what? Why was he fabricating their relationship for his brother? She wanted to ask him but Carla's curious gaze settled on them, as though she too was waiting to hear the answer.

Dario continued to hold her close as he addressed his brother. "Since when did you become my parent?"

Gianna finally came out of her shock at being called Dario's fiancée and found her voice.

"Franco, perhaps you'd like to join us. I have coffee or iced tea?"

The lines between Franco's brows deepened as he continued staring at his brother. "And you feel an engagement is a good enough reason to just leave your work behind and what?" For the first time Franco glanced around at the villa. "Stay here in your love shack?"

Love shack? What? No one talked about her beloved home like that. Those were fighting words. It might not be as fancy as other homes but it had its own charms. Gianna's narrowed gaze settled on Franco. "I'll have you know that this was my grandparents' home. It is no shack."

Franco blinked and glanced at her with a blank look, as though he'd been so focused on his brother that he'd forgotten she was even there.

Dario tightened his hold on her and raised his voice so his brother would hear each and every word that he uttered. "You've just insulted Gianna and her home. You may take verbal swipes at me but never her."

Franco's head lowered ever so slightly. And for a moment, he actually looked contrite. Then his gaze met hers. "I'm sorry. I didn't mean to slight your home. It looks lovely. Sometimes, well, most of the time my brother tries my patience."

Gianna sent a pleading look to her cousin, who looked utterly amused by the verbal battle being waged in front of them. Just then Tito came and leaned against Gianna's leg as though not sure what he should do now. Gianna finally caught Carla's attention and signaled with her eyes that she needed a little assistance to gain the brothers' attention. Carla nodded in understanding.

"I know," Carla said. "We'll have a private dinner this evening, you know, to celebrate the engagement."

Gianna shook her head. "No. I don't think that's a good idea."

"I'm sorry you feel that way," Franco said. "And it's my fault. I've given you a poor first impression and I apologize." His gaze met Gianna's. "I'm just a bit taken aback that my brother, who hates commitments, would settle down so suddenly."

Carla spoke up, "Maybe if you give my cousin a chance, you'd learn the reason your brother has changed his bachelor ways."

Franco nodded in agreement. He rubbed the back of his neck. "I'd like that." And then his gaze returned to Gianna. "I hope you'll give me another chance."

Gianna felt like the fly caught in the proverbial cobweb. No matter what she decided, she was in trouble. Either she went along with this outlandish ruse that Dario had concocted to obviously annoy his brother or she had to appear foolish and an utter failure in front of her cousin, whose respect meant the world to her.

"I don't know," Gianna said, looking to Dario for some help on getting out of an awkward evening where they'd obviously be found out. There was no way anyone would believe they were lovers. The truth was bound to come out.

"We have no plans," Dario said so nonchalantly that no one would ever suspect he'd spontaneously made up their whole relationship without even so much as consulting her. "Do we Gianna?"

She resisted the urge to glare at him. But when they were alone once more, she had a lot to say to him—a whole lot. He may write fiction but she didn't intend to get caught up in a fictional engagement with him.

"No. We don't."

And so their fate was sealed.

CHAPTER FIVE

H<small>E WASN'T HANDLING</small> this correctly.

Dario had been so caught off guard by his brother's sudden appearance that he'd reached for any excuse to explain his presence at the villa that had nothing to do with his writing. He didn't want his brother's negative thoughts about his pursuit of a writing career to infiltrate his mind. He already had enough of his own doubts about being able to pull off writing book number two.

One-hit wonder.

The taunt flitted through his mind. And his brother and family didn't even know about book one because Dario had insisted on using a pen name: D.J. March. If everyone hated his book, he hadn't wanted to embarrass his family, especially when the family business carried the same name. As shocking as it was, book one had become an international best seller.

He didn't know how the writing of book one could have flowed so easily and yet book two was a start-and-stop endeavor. *Dig deeper.* It's what his agent kept saying after reading a draft of book two. Dario didn't know if there was any deeper he could go.

Still, he shouldn't have dragged Gianna into this mess with him. It was enough that she'd opened her home to him. But pretending to be his fiancée was asking too much of her.

Dario cleared his throat. "I need to say something—"

"We both need to say something," Gianna interrupted. "We don't think the dinner is a good idea." When Carla's eyes widened in surprise, Gianna went on to add, "What I mean to say is we don't want to impose on you both. I'm sure Franco must have plans and Carla, you always have a busy social calendar."

It's not what Dario thought she was going to say. Why did she stop him from setting everyone straight about their relationship? And then a sinking feeling in his gut had him wondering if he'd read Gianna all wrong. Was she some sort of gold digger? Had she recognized the name of their family's company and realized Dario wasn't a struggling writer but an heir to a fortune?

A knot of worry tightened with each breath. His gaze moved to Gianna and he was tempted to say something here and now, but doing that would just confirm his brother's poor impression of him. No, he would wait until they were alone and then he'd sort this out.

Carla waved away any concerns about the impromptu dinner party. "It's no trouble at all. It's the least I can do for my cousin. And it'll just be the four of us as my father is about to leave on a business trip." Carla turned to Franco. "You'll join us, won't you?"

"I'm sure my brother has to get back to the city," Dario interjected, hoping Franco had more pressing matters in the city. "Don't you, Franco?"

"As a matter of fact, I've just completed my business—"

"Business here?" Dario didn't believe him. It was just an excuse to come here and check up on him, just like his brother had been doing most of his life.

Franco nodded. "Believe it or not, I don't have time to chase after you. The family business is at stake."

"You make it sound like it's in trouble. And that would never happen. Grandfather wouldn't stand for it."

"Shows how much you've been around the office lately."

"I haven't been gone that long." Just over a month. How much could happen in four weeks?

"Even when you were there, you weren't there. You're always distracted." Franco's gaze moved to Gianna. "Now I guess I know what, or should I say whom, had you so distracted."

Gianna pulled out of Dario's hold and stepped

toward his brother. "I can assure you that I'm no one's distraction." Her gaze narrowed on his brother. "I don't know you but you are certainly nothing like your brother."

"You mean because I have a solid work ethic—"

"No, because you are rather boorish."

Franco's eyes widened as his mouth opened slightly but no words came out.

Dario smiled. With each passing second, his smile broadened and then his amusement spilled over into laughter. He didn't think there was anyone in this world that could make his brother speechless.

Gianna spun around and nailed him with a sharp stare. "What are you laughing about?"

He quickly contained his amusement. "Nothing. Nothing at all."

He noticed how her blue eyes glittered when she was fired up. And here he thought he was the only one that let his brother get under his skin. Not that his brother was a bad guy—far from it. It's like their father used to say, the brothers mixed like oil and water.

Still, he wanted to know if Gianna had meant to come to his defense. Or if she had done it strictly out of self-defense. But as the question teetered on the tip of his tongue, he bit it back. Now wasn't the time for such probing questions—not with an avid audience.

He turned his attention back to his brother, who had smartly decided to quiet down. A smile pulled ever so slightly at the corners of Dario's lips. Perhaps keeping Gianna around wasn't such a bad idea after all. At least until he finished his book—if that ever happened.

Carla moved to Franco's side. "Perhaps we shouldn't have intruded on their private time."

Franco blinked as though her voice had drawn him from his thoughts. He glanced over at Carla and smiled. "I think you're right." Franco glanced back at Dario and Gianna. "I apologize for my unexpected arrival. Though I did try to call."

He had? Dario pulled his phone from his pocket and glanced at it to find more than two dozen missed calls. As he flipped to the call log, he was relieved to find that only a few were from his brother. A large number were from his agent. And then there were others from his editor at the publishing house. Everyone was getting anxious for the book—the book that he was certain, at this stage, would be an utter disappointment.

"I had my phone muted so it wouldn't interrupt me—" He halted his words. He was about to add while he was writing, but he'd caught himself in time.

"They want to be alone," Carla added as she slipped her hand into the crook of his brother's arm. "Perhaps we should go. We have plenty of time to catch up with them this evening."

His brother checked the time again. "You're right. We should go."

Carla smiled brightly. "Wonderful. I'll see everyone at my villa at seven. Don't be late." When both she and Franco turned to leave, Dario noticed that Carla was still holding onto his brother—who also didn't have time for a relationship. And yet his brother didn't seem to mind Carla's company. Interesting.

"Now, where do you live?" Franco's voice faded as they headed back toward the drive.

The time of reckoning had come. Dario swallowed hard and then turned to face Gianna. "I'm sorry about all that. I had absolutely no idea he'd track me down here."

She turned her back to him as she moved toward the table with Tito by her side. "You don't have to apologize."

"But I do. I dragged you into this—this *fake* relationship—without even asking you." He'd stressed the word fake to see if it'd get a reaction from her. It didn't. Thankfully. Because he wasn't about to let her think anything would ever happen between them.

"As I recall, it was my cousin who got us into this fine mess." She moved to the kitchen, but then quickly returned with her hands full.

They both sat down at the table. Gianna poured them each a glass of freshly squeezed lemonade from the homegrown lemons in her side yard.

Dario raked his fingers through his hair. "Tonight we have to be honest with them and explain the misunderstanding."

Gianna arched a brow. "Are you willing to tell your brother what you're really doing here?"

Dario's lips pressed into a firm line as he shook his head. He needed to keep it a secret from his family for just a little longer—just until he finished these revisions—revisions that just might be the death of him. He just couldn't wrap his mind around what he needed to do to make this book as good—no, better—than the last one.

"Then I propose we make a deal."

He wasn't sure he liked where this was going, but he had to admit she'd spiked his curiosity. "I'm listening."

"How about for the next month we let my cousin and your brother believe we're engaged?"

"I don't know—"

"It'll give you the time you need to finish your book."

That was much as true. "But what will you get out of it?"

"I'd like to be the one to end the relationship."

"And why would you want to do that?"

"So my cousin doesn't pity me and think I can't keep a man—even if it's the truth." Pain showed in her eyes.

Whoever had dumped her was a fool. Sure, he hadn't known her long but from what he could see she had a kind heart, she defended those she considered her friends and, well, he liked her—though merely as a friend, nothing more.

How could he refuse her request, when it would help him the most? The thought of being dumped, fictional or not, would be a blow to his ego. But it was a price he was willing to pay to make his dream of being a true and honest author and not the one-hit wonder that his agent had mentioned in passing as a possibility.

Dario extended his hand to her. It was already out there when he recalled their prior handshake and how it'd affected him. But surely he'd blown that out of proportion.

Her brow scrunched up. "What are you doing?"

"You wanted to make a deal, right?" When she nodded, he continued, "Then we need to shake on it to make it official."

She hesitated. "News of our engagement won't go any further than the four of us, right?"

"Absolutely. After all, I'm not looking forward to getting dumped publicly."

Her gaze met his as though judging if he was telling the truth or not. Then she placed her soft hand in his. With her blue gaze still holding his, he wrapped his fingers around her hand and gave a slight squeeze.

As he continued to hold her hand a little longer than was necessary, a sense of awareness pulsed up his arm and set his heart beating faster.

There it was again—that strong sense of attraction. He suddenly wondered if pretending to be in love with this beautiful woman was going to be harder than he'd ever imagined.

Gianna withdrew her hand and glanced away. Was it possible that she'd sensed his desire where she was concerned? He definitely needed to keep his hands to himself for the next month.

CHAPTER SIX

ONE MONTH.

Well, not quite.

Four entire weeks.

Twenty-eight very long days.

No matter which way Gianna phrased it, it still sounded like forever. What exactly had she gotten herself into?

As Gianna dressed for dinner that evening, her stomach shivered with nerves. What had she been thinking to perpetuate this preposterous notion that she and Dario were in love? After all, they hardly knew each other.

The breath caught in her throat. There was no way they were going to get through this dinner without the two people closest to them figuring out that this was one big charade.

In the next breath, she realized she couldn't just blurt out at dinner that it was all a lie. Then her cousin would know how foolish she'd been to fall for someone she worked with—someone who'd just broken up with someone else—and that she'd rebounded straight into a fake relationship. Even to her own ears, it sounded pathetic. Maybe there was a way they could pull off this fake engagement. After all, it was only dinner.

Gianna moved faster. After showering, styling her shoulder-length hair and applying a modest amount of makeup, she only had to pick out a dress. How hard could that be?

Her first choice was a little black dress. After all, it was her go-to outfit. But as she held it in front of her, she frowned. There was absolutely nothing summery about it. And the color was all wrong to celebrate a new love and engagement.

Gianna dug to the back of her closet where she had some summer dresses she'd bought at an end-of-the-season sale. There was a sky blue one, an aqua one and a white one. Each had a different cut. One by one, she held them in front of her, turning this way and that way in front of the mirror. It was so hard to choose. But a traditional bride's color was white so that's the one she chose.

With the dress on, she slipped on some heels and rushed out to the pool area and headed straight for the guesthouse. The door was open as usual, but she didn't want to intrude. Instead, she stood outside and knocked on the wood trim. "Dario, we need to go. Are you almost ready?"

"I've been ready for some time." The voice came from behind her.

She turned to find Dario sitting in a chair in the shadows with Tito lying next to him. "Why didn't you say something when you saw me rush across the patio?"

He shrugged. "You seemed to be in such a hurry that I was curious what was up."

"And so you sat quietly watching."

"Something like that." He glanced at his Rolex, which looked strikingly similar to his brother's. "But you know we still have a good fifteen minutes until we have to leave."

She sat down at the table. "We have a problem."

His expression turned serious. "Are you thinking of backing out of our deal? Because we did shake on it."

"No. Well, not exactly."

His brow crinkled with worry lines. "What exactly is it?"

"They're going to figure out that we're not a couple."

"What makes you think that? They were certainly eager enough to believe it earlier."

"But that was different. We weren't sitting down at dinner, carrying on a conversation. And they weren't asking us questions. They'll quickly figure out we don't know the first thing about each other." She clenched her hands together to keep from nervously fidgeting with her teardrop pearl pendant.

"Ah, but that's not quite true."

"It isn't?"

He smiled and shook his head. "I know your most painful secret and you happen to know my most prized wish. And those are two things that no one else knows about us."

Heat crept into her cheeks. "But you know my secret because I had an embarrassing meltdown in front of you."

"Doesn't matter how you told me. The fact is you did tell me."

"And you only told me about your book because you were trying to convince me to let you stay here."

"Again, the circumstances don't matter."

She frowned at him. "Has anyone ever told you that you can be quite contrary?"

"No. But I bet if you mention it to my brother that he'll agree with you." Dario sent her a charming smile that made her stomach dip, and for a moment, she forgot her worries.

She smiled. "You know I think you're right about that one."

"So what would you like to know about me before we go to dinner?" He once more checked the time. "You have precisely eleven minutes to learn my life story."

"That isn't much time."

He averted his eyes. "There really isn't that much to know."

She had the feeling there was a whole lot to know, but he wasn't anxious to pry open the closed door and reveal his skeletons. She couldn't blame him. She wasn't so anxious herself. "Maybe we could just start with the little things."

"Such as?"

"Your favorite color? Your birthday? Where did you go to school? You know, those sorts of things that every fiancée should know about their partner."

His favorite color was blue whereas hers was purple. He was four years older than her. And he attended college in the States like she'd done. The difference was that he'd earned a business degree on the East Coast while she'd gone to film school on the West Coast.

The more they talked the more she could see the possibility of them being real friends and not just temporary housemates. But they didn't have long to talk and so no deep dark secrets were revealed by either of them. And she wondered what he had to hide. Surely, it couldn't be as bad as her romantic past.

A candlelit dinner for four.

A terrace that overlooked Lake Como.

Boy. Girl. Boy. Girl. It was really rather cozy.

A gentle breeze brushed over Gianna's bare arms, easing the warmth from the slowly sinking sun. She'd moved the food around her plate more than she'd eaten it. The truth was her stomach was tied up in a big knot.

"Let's see the ring," Carla said with excitement.

Gianna stared down at her bare ring finger. She wasn't sure how to explain the absence of a ring.

Dario spoke up. "She doesn't have it."

"You didn't buy your fiancée a ring before asking her to marry you?" Franco frowned at him.

Gianna jumped to Dario's defense. "Of course, he did. It's just that it's too big and kept falling off. We have to get it sized."

"So how did you two meet?" Carla's gaze moved between the two of them.

Gianna's body tensed. This was the question she'd been expecting and the absolute last question she wanted to answer. It was part of the reason she'd been unusually talkative that evening, hoping to divert attention away from them. Gianna's gaze moved to Dario. He stared blankly back at her. *Oh, no. He's going to be no help.*

Gianna turned back to her cousin. "You don't want to hear that story. It's boring."

"I highly doubt that." Carla's eyes zeroed in on her with intense interest. Her cousin was a romantic at heart. "I definitely want to hear the details. Did he sweep you right off your feet?"

Gianna felt cornered. She knew what her cousin was like when she was on to something.

She wouldn't let up until she got the details. Panic sent her heart racing.

"We met here in Gemma." Gianna's mind scrambled for details that eluded her.

"That's right," Dario chimed in. His gaze caught and held hers. "It was a nice weekend and I needed to get away from the city."

"And I was between shoots so I was home. I was walking home from the village when this dog came strolling down the road toward me." Gianna continued staring into Dario's warm brown eyes. "He seemed so sweet and lost."

"Tito was leading me toward my future," Dario said and for the briefest second, Gianna wanted to believe him. "He'd gotten away from me when we were walking down by the lake."

"But he found me and followed me home." Gianna smiled as she recalled her first meeting with Tito.

"But how in the world did Dario find you both?" Carla's voice drew Gianna from her thoughts.

She glanced over to find Carla with her chin propped up by the palm of her hand as she ate up each word they were dishing up. Gianna chanced a glance at Franco. He was leaning back in his chair with his arms crossed. His dark eyes didn't betray his thoughts. She could only hope he was buying what they were selling.

Dario reached out, placing his hand over hers.

The warmth of his touch caused her heart to beat faster. And when her gaze once more met his, her stomach fluttered.

He smiled broadly, showing off his adorable dimples. "That's where serendipity played a part. Because I obviously wasn't leaving without Tito."

"And I needed to find his owner."

"So Gianna called me. As soon as I heard her voice, I knew there was something special about her."

Gianna smiled. "You did not."

"I did." He said the words so earnestly that even she wanted to believe him. "I asked her to meet me at a small café here in the village. And as soon as I saw her, I was a goner."

Heat swirled in her chest and rushed up her neck, setting her cheeks aflame. He was saying all the words she'd longed for a man to say to her. And in the moment, she wanted it all to be true.

And then he leaned toward her. *What is he doing?* He kept moving closer, all the while his thumb stroked the back of her hand. Her heart beat erratically.

Was he—was he going to kiss her? Her heart leaped into her throat. Anticipation thrummed in her veins. As his lips hovered over hers, her eyes fluttered shut.

He pressed his mouth to hers. Time stood still. Reality slipped away as they encompassed this alternate universe where they allowed themselves to enjoy the kiss that had been inevitable since their first meeting.

She savored the firm press of his mouth to hers—the gentle touch of his fingers over hers. This kiss shouldn't be this good—this stirring. She was over men. She was focusing solely on her career. But would it hurt to savor this very brief moment? A moan swelled in her throat. She tamped it down.

And then he pulled back. A huge smile lit up his handsome face and made his brown eyes sparkle in the candlelight. He gave her hand a squeeze before releasing it. What did that squeeze mean? Was he trying to tell her something? Had the kiss affected him as much as it had her? Her pulse was still racing.

As he turned to say something to his brother, Gianna blinked. She resisted the urge to run a finger over her tingling lips. Had that really happened? Had he kissed her like a lover?

Oh, yes, he had. But it was all just a show. That was it. Nothing more. Right? Because neither one of them were into relationships. And the more she got to know him, the more she liked him—as a friend.

And then she remembered how quickly her last relationship had started for all the wrong reasons. She wasn't about to repeat that mistake.

Her heart slowed its pace. She wouldn't let herself get drawn in. Not again.

With that in mind, she swallowed hard before turning her attention back to the conversation at hand. What were they discussing? She had totally lost track of what was being said.

"I admit I had my doubts about the two of you," Franco said, "but no one can fake a kiss like that one."

"I agree," Carla said. "You two were made for each other."

"Can you do us a favor?" Gianna asked. "Can you keep the engagement to yourselves for a little while? We wanted to get the ring sized before we started telling people."

Both Carla and Franco seemed a bit surprised by the request, but they agreed.

The conversation moved to talk about Franco wanting Dario to return to the office to cover for him. Dario refused to leave. He said he would handle whatever came up remotely. And Gianna was left trying to pretend that the kiss had never happened. Someone should be filming this because she certainly deserved an award for her acting skills.

CHAPTER SEVEN

Cocktails. Check.
  Dinner. Check.
  Kiss. Double-check.
Dario smiled as he and Gianna got ready to leave. The truth was that he'd actually enjoyed himself tonight. He hadn't relaxed around his brother in a very long time. And it was all thanks to Gianna. She'd made it possible to see his brother as a friend again. He knew it wouldn't last, but he was grateful for the evening.

And then there was that kiss. He wouldn't mind repeating it. It had been much sweeter than the tiramisu they'd had for dessert. And so much more addictive.

But he knew the danger in getting drawn in by someone. His mother was on her third—he paused to think about it—yes, her third marriage. She was still hoping someone else could make her happy. It never worked out.

Secretly, he thought his mother was still hung up on their father. But that was a lost cause. His father couldn't commit to living in one place for a year much less commit to a relationship. It just wasn't in his DNA.

And Dario believed he was a lot like his father. He looked like him—so everyone said—and he couldn't commit to anything, be it the family business or a relationship. At least he'd recognized this early on, before destroying the lives of a devoted wife and two adoring kids.

Still, he would continue to play the part of Gianna's fiancé so long as they both realized it was all fiction, including the kiss—especially the kiss. This would soon be over. He would hopefully move on with his publishing dreams and Gianna would move on to working for a new television show, leaving no lingering strings between them.

Carla smiled. "That was a lovely evening. We'll have to do this again."

Dario struggled not to smile. He was home free. Their little charade had worked. By the time he saw his brother again, hopefully his revisions would be complete and approved by both his agent and editor. Oh, and his sudden engagement would have ended as suddenly as it had begun. Other than his brother and Gianna's cousin, no one would know about their ever so brief engagement.

"What are you smiling about?" Franco looked directly at him.

He was smiling? He supposed he was as he felt rather proud of himself. Still, he didn't want his brother pushing for the source of his pleasure. He schooled his face into a nonchalant expression. "I didn't realize I was smiling."

"Mind sharing what has made you so happy?"

Carla patted Franco's arm. "He's in love. What more is there to say?"

Franco sighed before nodding in agreement. Dario could sense his brother wasn't as on board with this engagement as he'd like people to think. Did it bother Franco that Gianna didn't run in the same circles as their family? What else could he object to? Gianna was beautiful, friendly and fun to be around.

Franco turned to Dario. "It'd be helpful if you were back at the office while I'm out of town."

So that's what was eating at his brother. He was relieved it had nothing to do with Gianna.

Dario shook his head. He was standing firm about not returning to the office until he'd completed his book.

"I'm sorry," Gianna spoke up. "He promised he'd help me with a special project."

Everyone's gazes turned in her direction. Dario had to wonder what she was up to this time. They hadn't discussed any special project, had they? He searched his memory. No, they hadn't. He wouldn't forget something like that.

"Special project," Carla said, "That sounds interesting."

Franco cleared his throat. "What sort of special project?"

Dario's thoughts echoed the words of his brother. What did she have in mind for him? Whatever she'd come up with, he hoped it was just a story to get him off the hook as far as going back to the office because he had to stay focused on the book.

"You know how I told you I'm a camerawoman?" When Franco nodded, she continued. "Well, I'm also into still life photography. There's a photography competition coming up and I plan to enter it."

She did? This was news to Dario. Although, just about everything about her was news to him. Still, there was something about the conviction in her voice and the gleam in her eyes that told him this was more than just a cover story to help him out. She was quite serious about entering.

Franco's brow arched. "The one at the Botanical Gardens?"

Gianna smiled and nodded. "The very one."

"What will be your focus?"

She continued to smile as she shook her head. "I can't tell you that. After all, I don't want anyone to steal my idea."

Franco nodded. "Understood. I suppose I should be going. I have a number of phone calls to return when I get back to my room and I have to hit the road early in the morning."

"It was so nice meeting you," Gianna said. "I hope we get to meet again."

"Of course we will. You're marrying my brother."

Color bloomed in Gianna's cheeks. "Of course. What I meant to say is that I hope we see each other soon."

"We will."

"We will?" Dario asked, wondering if his brother was planning another impromptu visit.

"Yes." Franco's gaze met his. "Have you forgotten Nonno and Nonna's anniversary party?"

He had.

"No, I haven't. But I can't recall what day they selected for the dinner."

"Oh. It's no longer just a dinner. It's going to be a full-fledged party that lasts all weekend."

"Sounds very impressive," Gianna said.

"It definitely will be. This is their sixtieth wedding anniversary. It'll be a chance for you to meet the extended family." Franco gave his brother a brief hug. When Gianna held her hand out to him, he smiled. He ignored her offer of a handshake and instead hugged her too—just like she was family. He paused in front of Carla, took her hand and kissed the back of it. "Thank you for such a lovely evening. Now, I really must go."

"I'm sorry everyone has to leave so soon,"

Carla said. "I suppose we all must be responsible adults. Although, wouldn't it be fun for once to party the night away and sleep until lunchtime like when we were kids?"

They all agreed before making their way to the driveway.

Dario opened the car door for Gianna. Once he climbed in the driver's seat, he started the car and off they drove into the dusky evening.

"That went better than I thought it would go," he said. "Other than your cousin, we should be in the clear."

"You don't think your brother will be back to check up on us?"

He shook his head while keeping his gaze on the road as they passed through the village. Many of the locals were still out and about enjoying the summer evening. "No. My brother has one focus—the business. It's the only reason he was here. He wanted me back in the office. The thing is, I don't feel needed there. My grandfather, who is supposed to be retiring, still stays involved. Sure, I'm a Marchello and I can sign the checks but, well, I want to contribute something unique to this world—something that's solely me." He slowed to a stop at an intersection. He glanced over at her. "Is that wrong?"

"No. Not at all. And I guess in a way that's what I'm doing behind the camera. Even though

I'm portraying someone or something else, it's still my perspective that frames the footage."

For the first time ever, he felt as though he'd just gained an ally. He smiled. "Thanks."

"For what? I didn't do anything."

"You did more than you think." He checked the intersection and then proceeded toward home—his temporary home.

The evening had gone much better than he'd expected and it was just early enough that he would be able to get some more writing done. But he didn't know what to write—not yet. And the thought of staring at a blank page soured his good mood.

"What's wrong?" Gianna's voice drew him from his troubling thoughts.

"What did you say?"

"You were frowning. You know you don't have to lie to me. You can admit if you hated the evening."

He shook his head as his thoughts rewound back to the moment of their kiss. He shouldn't have done it. At first, he had thought of it to get his brother off his back with his little quips, but then as he'd turned to Gianna and his gaze had settled on her glossy lips, he'd forgotten all about his brother. His focus had been solely on her. She was beautiful. He'd thought that the first time he'd met her and since then he'd come to find that her beauty started on the inside and worked its way out.

So when it came to kissing her, he couldn't resist. The idea had tempted and teased him until he had to know what it'd be like to feel her shimmery lips pressed to his. His imagined kiss had been good, but it was nothing compared to the real thing.

It was for that very reason that it couldn't happen again. Gianna wasn't one to be trifled with as she'd already had her heart broken. And he couldn't offer her the things that were important to her: love, commitment, marriage and a family.

Just the thought of being trapped in a relationship knotted him up on the inside. It was best to forget the playacting and get back to being housemates. Nothing more.

"Trust me, I wasn't frowning about the evening. I thought that it went well. So much better than I ever would have imagined."

"Then what's bothering you?"

He sighed. He hadn't intended to get into this with her. But after the bond they'd formed by covering for each other, he couldn't just brush her off now. "I was thinking about my book."

"And it made you frown?"

He nodded. "It needs changes and I'm struggling with them. It's why I needed the extra month here at the villa. I need to get it revised and submitted before I head back to the city and get distracted with business."

"And it's not going well?"

"I'm stuck. There's something missing from the book and I just can't figure out what it is. I didn't have this problem with *The Rise of Lavar*."

"That's your book?" When he nodded, she said, "I loved it! I had no idea you wrote it."

His face grew warm. "You don't have to say that."

"I mean it. I lost sleep reading it. It was a real page-turner."

She was the first person to say that to him, aside from his agent and editor. It felt really good.

"I can't believe you read my book."

"I was hoping there'd be a second book."

"I'm hoping the same thing."

"I'm sorry you're having problems with it, but you'll figure it out."

He pulled to a stop in the driveway in front of the villa. He turned off the engine and then turned to her. "I wouldn't be so certain. I have a deadline at the end of the month. One way or another, I have to turn in what I have and take my chances with the publisher."

"They won't reject it."

His brows rose. "You sound awfully confident. You haven't even read it."

She smiled. "If it's anything like the first book, it'll be another best seller."

He was still having a hard time believing she'd chosen his book to read out of the millions of books available. "Did you really read it?"

"Since you seem to have a hard time believing it, I'll prove it." She dashed out of the car and made her way into the house.

He followed her. All the while, he was smiling. She really liked his writing before she even knew who he was. His chest puffed up ever so slightly and his chin rose a notch. He had to finish this rewrite—if not for himself, then for Gianna. His first official fan. That sounded so strange to him.

She met up with him on the patio and held up a paperback copy of the book. "See. I told you I read it. And if you still don't believe me, look at the bent spine. There might even be a coffee stain or two."

He continued to smile as he accepted the well-read book. "And you really liked it?" He just had to be certain. For some reason, her opinion really mattered to him. "You're not just saying it to be nice to me? Not that you have a reason to be nice to me—"

"Stop." She smiled at him. "Yes, I'm being totally serious. I loved the book. You made the world of Lavar so real. I could see it all in my mind."

"You could?" The problem with being a writer in hiding was that you never got to talk to people face-to-face about your work. And agents and editors don't count. But Gianna was neither. She was just a reader—a reader whose opinion mattered a lot to him.

She laughed. "You aren't very good at taking compliments, are you?"

He shrugged. He wasn't used to receiving them.

"You did a wonderful job with the descriptions. And the hero's journey to becoming the head of the Lavarians was impressive. I didn't see the end coming."

"Neither did I. It sort of wrote itself."

"Really?"

He nodded. "I had a loose outline but then the characters took over and told their own story."

"That must have been exciting. I love surprises." The smile slipped from her face. "Well, most surprises. The good kind. Not the I'm-dumping-you-and-going-back-to-my-ex kind."

He felt bad for her. "I wouldn't like that surprise either."

They continued to discuss his book. And he surprised himself by being so open about it. The things he thought really worked in the book, the things he'd wished he thought to include and the parts that just didn't come across the way he wanted them to. But overall, he was very happy with the final result.

"The thing about this second book is my agent says it isn't different enough from the first."

"I'm sorry. I wish I could help."

"Thanks. I keep thinking of what to change but so far none of it works. It just feels off, if you know what I mean. Like it's being forced."

"If you want, I could read it and see if I have any ideas." She waggled her brows as though enticing him to agree.

He couldn't help but laugh. "If I didn't know better, I'd think you were just finding an excuse to read the next book before anyone else."

"Would that be so bad?"

"No. But I don't want to disappoint you."

"You won't."

"That's what you say now but you haven't read the book yet."

"So let me." She clasped her hands together and sent him a pleading look. "Please. All this talk about it has me dying to know what happens next."

He was torn. Part of him said that an unbiased opinion would be helpful. But the other part of him didn't want Gianna disappointed with his book—with him. If she hated it, there would be an awkwardness between them. He didn't want that to happen. He was just getting used to their friendship.

He was about to turn her down when he recalled how much she'd helped him with his brother and given him this month to revisit the book. He couldn't afford to squander the time.

And she was truly offering to help him without asking for anything in return. He would be a fool to turn her down.

"Okay," he said. "Do you prefer print or digital?"

Her face lit up like a kid's on Christmas morning. "Digital because I'm going to be taking it to bed with me."

Suddenly, he was disappointed to know it was just his book she was taking to bed. As soon as the thought came to him, he dismissed it. He couldn't let that one impulsive kiss distract him into thinking they'd ever share more. Even if the thought was tempting… So deliciously tempting.

It couldn't happen because he refused to hurt her. And he would eventually. Of that he was certain.

"Dario?" Gianna waved her hand in front of his face. "Hey, where did you go?"

"To bed." Suddenly, his face felt warm, and when she sent him a puzzled look, he swallowed hard and said, "I mean it's time to go to bed." As an after-thought, he added, "Alone." He got to his feet and started for the guesthouse. He called out over his shoulder, "I'll send you the file."

"But you don't even have my email address."

He stopped and smothered a groan. The last thing he needed was to spend more time with her. The longer he was around her, the more his thoughts drifted into dangerous territory. Still, he couldn't ignore her.

He turned back to her. "Sorry. I forgot."

"I'll just jot it down for you." Without waiting for him to respond, she rushed into the main house. A minute later, she returned with a bright orange slip of paper. She held it out to him. "Here you go."

When he went to take it from her, their fingers touched. A now familiar electric current rushed up his arm and then down his spine. His whole body was awakened.

His gaze met hers. He forgot what he'd been about to say. His heart pounded so loud that he was certain she could hear it.

He should look away. He should move. He should do something. Anything.

And then his gaze dipped to her lips. They shimmered in the moonlight. It was as though they were tempting him—teasing him. After all, it wouldn't be their first kiss. What would it hurt to follow that seemingly innocent kiss with another one—one with more heat, more passion and more desire?

Gianna yanked back her hand. "I better make a cup of tea to take to bed."

He just stood there wordlessly because his brain and mouth were at a total disconnect. He watched the gentle sway of her hips as she walked away. His mouth grew dry. He swallowed hard. It was all he could do not to go after her.

It wasn't until she disappeared around a corner

that the spell was broken. He blinked and turned away. What in the world had happened there? It was though she'd bewitched him with just the touch of her hand. But that was impossible. He may write fantasy but that didn't mean he believed in it. Still, something kept happening between them. He just wasn't prepared to analyze it. They were friends. Nothing more.

CHAPTER EIGHT

Buzz-buzz.

Gianna groaned. Her eyelids lifted a fraction to check the caller ID. She didn't recognize it. The brightness of the sun had her eyelids slamming back shut. The darkness welcomed her. She was so tired and sleep felt so good. Just a little longer…

Buzz-buzz.

She groaned again but this time she opened one eye to see the bright sunshine streaming in through the window. To be that bright out, it had to mean she'd slept in. Her other eye fluttered open. When she rolled over, her e-reader slipped from her chest and clattered to the floor.

Gianna groaned once more. She hoped this wasn't an omen of what was to come this day. Lucky for her, she'd bought a protective cover for it. She must have fallen asleep while reading. She picked it up and then placed it next to the bed. That's when she noticed her bedside lamp was still on.

She'd been so caught up in reading Dario's book last night that she hadn't wanted to stop, even when her eyes had grown heavy. She grabbed her e-reader and opened it. She was only 48 percent of the way through the book and she couldn't wait to finish it. But first she had work to do.

In her free time, she'd been adding photos to a stock image site. It didn't make her a lot of money, but now that she'd quit her job, every little bit helped. She liked to do nature scenes. And she'd been hoping to capture the sunrise over Lake Como, but she'd totally missed it that day.

Still, there was a meadow not far from her house and it had the most beautiful wildflowers every year. She was hoping they were in full bloom. She'd been serious the other night about entering the photography competition. And once she snapped some photos, she'd come back here and continue reading.

In no time, she was dressed and ready to go. Her first stop was her office in the back of the house. She turned on her computer and then brought up the website for the photography competition. The deadline to enter was tomorrow night. She filled out the form and paid the staggering entry fee.

She printed out the instructions. She noted two dates on her digital calendar. The first date was when the prints had to be received. The second date was the day of judging. It was at the end of the month. She told herself she had plenty of time to come up with the winning entry, but she felt rushed. However, she always did like a challenge.

She shut down her computer and rushed to the kitchen. She grabbed some fruit, bread and cheese, and placed it all in her backpack. Armed with her camera, she headed out past the pool.

Woof. Woof.

With his tail wagging, Tito rushed up to her. A smile pulled at her lips as she bent down to pet him. "What are you up to this morning?"

Woof.

"I'm not sure what you want." She glanced around for Dario, but he appeared to be inside the guesthouse, probably working on his revisions. "I'm sorry, Tito. But I have to go."

She gave him a final pat and started to walk away. He proceeded to follow her. She stopped and he stopped. She smiled as he gazed up at her with those big brown eyes.

"You can't come with me. Dario will miss you." She supposed she would have to be a little firmer with him. She lowered her voice, hoping it sounded more commanding. "Stay."

Tito lowered his head and whined as though he didn't know what he'd done wrong. It pulled on her heartstrings.

She knelt down and hugged him. "I'm sorry. Maybe next time."

She started toward the back of the property. When she paused to look over her shoulder, Tito was a few steps behind her. He stopped and then looked at the ground.

A big smile pulled at her lips. If Tito didn't already belong to Dario, she'd adopt him. He was such a sweetie. What would it hurt to take him with her?

She backtracked. "Okay, we'll check with Dario and see if he'll let you go with me. Would you like that?"

Woof.

"Aw…see, I know what you're saying this time."

At the guesthouse, she rapped her knuckles on the door. "Dario?"

"Coming." There were some shuffling sounds, a crash and a mutter. Then the door opened. "Sorry. I ran into the corner of the table. But don't worry. Nothing is broken. The table I mean, not me."

She continued to smile as she took in his disheveled appearance. His hair was once again mussed. There were shadows under his eyes as though he hadn't slept much last night either. And there was scruff along his jawline.

He cleared his throat. "Are you here to talk about the book?"

presence—with her glowing smile and the pleasant lilt of her voice.

They walked a bit. All the while, Tito was pulling on his retractable leash. The pup was eager to smell everything.

Meanwhile, Gianna had grown quiet, lost in her own world, leaving him to his own meandering thoughts. Then she'd suddenly stop. She'd study something in the distance. He'd tried peering over her shoulder to find out what was so interesting. Each time he did it, he didn't see anything special. To him, it all appeared just to be some dirt, foliage or trees.

However, Gianna had amazing sight. Where he'd see nothing but an old log, she'd see a log with green moss and a white butterfly. And when she showed him a preview of the photo, he was in awe.

"You're really good at this photography stuff."

"Thanks. It's a hobby."

"A hobby? You should make it your occupation. I can envision those prints ending up on peoples' walls." He intended to buy some for his apartment if she made them available.

Her cheeks pinkened. "You don't have to say that."

"But it's the truth. Those are at least as good as the prints in your house."

Her gaze searched his. "You really think so?"

She had been hoping to avoid him until she'd had a chance to finish reading it. "The book, um, no."

His dark brows drew together as disappointment clouded his eyes. "That bad?"

"Oh, no. That isn't what I meant. I guess I'm a slow reader but there's no way I could read it all last night." She thought of ditching her plans for the day and reading the rest of his book. As soon as the thought came to her, she realized that's what her former self would do. But this new her had to stay focused on her future. "I really liked what I read—"

"You did?"

She smiled and nodded. "You're a very talented writer."

"So then you don't think it needs massive revisions?"

"I... I didn't say that."

"Then you agree with my agent that something big is missing."

"I didn't say that either." She could see the worry written all over his face. "I just need to finish reading the book before I share my thoughts."

"Okay. You know you don't have to finish reading it if you don't want to."

"I know. But I really have to see how it ends. Anyway, I didn't mean to keep you," she said. "I just wanted to know if it'd be all right if I took Tito for a walk."

Tito moved to her side and sat down. And then he leaned his body against her leg.

"Looks like you totally won him over," Dario said.

"It's more like the other way around. I can't tell you how much food he's mooched from me with those big brown eyes. I don't know how you can resist him."

"I can't. That's why it's fine if he wants to go with you. By the way, where are you going?"

"For a hike. I want to take some photos. I know of this meadow not far away that has the most colorful wildflowers." And then a thought came to her. "Would you like to go with us?"

Dario raked his fingers through his hair. "I'm not exactly dressed to go out."

"Trust me. Where we're going, no one will see you. Unless you're worried about some wildlife wondering if you're one of them."

"Hey." He sent her a sheepish look. "Am I that bad?"

"Let's just say you look like you've been up all night."

"Not all night but a good portion of it. And how about you?"

She knew what he was asking. He wanted to know if she'd stayed up last night reading his book. "I was up very late. That's why I'm getting such a late start on the day."

"It's only a little past eight."

"Exactly. I like to be up with the sun."

He dramatically rolled his eyes. "You're starting to sound like my brother now."

She pressed a hand to her chest. "I'm wounded." She sent him a teasing smile. "Do I really sound that bad?"

"Maybe not that bad." Dario smiled for the first time that morning. "Give me a second to brush my teeth and make myself presentable. And I need to grab Tito's leash." He didn't wait for her response as he rushed back inside.

She turned back to Tito. "Looks like we're all going for a walk. If I didn't know better, I'd think that's what you had in mind all along."

Why had she offered to take Dario with them? It wasn't like they had to spend more time together. Their one night of engaged bliss was over. Carla was busy proving to her father that she was more than capable of taking over the family business. And Franco was out of the country. The charade was over. So why had she suggested spending the day with Dario?

He shouldn't be here.

He should be working.

And yet, Dario couldn't bring himself to turn around and go home. He told himself it was the sunshine and fresh air that had him feeling totally revived, and it had nothing to do with Gianna's

"I do. Trust me. I'm a Marchello. We are raised to be honest."

She smiled at him. "Except in the case of our engagement?"

"Okay. So there are exceptions. But I was serious. Those prints at the house are really good. Did you take them?"

"No. My grandmother was a photographer. I guess that's how I got caught up in it."

"But instead you spend most of your time filming documentaries?"

She nodded. "I like that too. I've been to some amazing places like the Himalayas, the Australian Outback and the Amazon."

His eyes widened. "That's some résumé. What's next?"

"I don't know." Her gaze lowered. "I broke a rule and mixed business with pleasure. And there was no way I could continue to work with my ex. My agent is searching for a new position and in the meantime, I sell stock images on the side while I prepare for the competition."

"I meant with your personal life." His gaze dipped to her lips—one of the reasons he hadn't gotten much sleep the night before. "Will you dump me for some good-looking guy?"

She laughed. A soft melodious sound. It was something that put him at ease. It made him forget that their romantic relationship was no more real that the characters in his book. And yet, he couldn't turn away from her. He was totally and completely drawn in.

"Go ahead and admit it," he coaxed. "I'm the best boyfriend ever."

Her eyes sparkled with amusement. "Yes, you are. Because you're not real."

He feigned a scowl. "I am too."

She was still smiling and now she was shaking her head. "No, you're not."

"I am and I can prove it." Without giving thought to his actions and instead totally living in the moment, he leaned toward her.

She pressed a hand to his chest and attempted to step back. "Dario…"

Gianna started to fall. He reached out to her in the nick of time, drawing her to him. Her soft curves pressed firmly against him.

"What in the world?" She looked down.

He did the same. It appeared while they were having a war of words, Tito was busy walking in a circle, ensnaring them with his leash. And now Tito was sitting with his back to them as though saying I got you two together, now you have to do the rest.

"We have to get untangled," Gianna said.

"Do we?"

Her gaze swung around and met his. "What are you saying?"

He continued to hold her in his arms, not because she needed the support but rather because he liked the way she felt there. He stared deep into her eyes. And when he spoke, his voice came out much deeper than normal. "Isn't it obvious?"

Her pouty lips opened but no words came out. She pressed them back together, but her eyes darkened with desire. A lopsided smile tugged at the corner of his mouth. He wasn't in this alone. What would it hurt to revisit that kiss from last night?

He needed to know if she was as sweet as he remembered. It'd taken every bit of willpower for him to restrain himself in front of his brother and her cousin. But out here, in the middle of nowhere, there was only Tito to watch them. And right now, his dog had given them a moment of privacy. And Dario intended to take full advantage of it.

His head lowered. He heard her inhale a quick breath. He was certain Gianna was about to rebuff his advance. But then his lips met hers. She didn't move, as though stunned by the action. It surely couldn't be that surprising.

They may not be a real couple—an engaged couple—but there were sparks and chemistry flaring between them. And if he didn't prove to himself that it was all flash with no substance, he'd never be able to concentrate on his revisions— revisions that still had him baffled.

But right now, as his lips moved over Gianna's,

he wasn't confused. He knew exactly what he wanted—more of her. His worries about his book slipped to the back of his mind. As the kiss deepened, he pulled her closer to him. Her hands landed on his chest. The heat of her touch radiated through his shirt and set his skin afire.

Her mouth opened to him, letting him delve inside. Instead of proving that he'd made too much of the kiss at dinner, he realized the real thing was so much more enticing—so much hotter.

Her fingers slipped up over his shoulders and wrapped around the back of his neck. She pulled him closer. The blood pounded in his veins. He'd never shared a kiss like this before. It was so addictive—

Woof. Woof-woof.

And then there was a jerk on the leash. Their lips parted. Tito continued to bark and pull on the leash. In the distance was a hare. It paused to look at Tito and then it hopped off into the green foliage. Tito continued to bark and yank on the leash.

It took Dario a moment to come back to his senses. He leaned over and grabbed hold of the leash. "Stop." When the dog didn't listen, he gave a quick tug on the leash as he raised his voice. "Tito, no."

The dog quieted and sat down but he kept his gaze focused on the last place he'd seen the hare.

The easiest thing would be to release Tito from

his leash until they unwound themselves, but he knew as soon as the dog was off the leash that he'd hightail it after the hare. Dario had no intention of spending the rest of the day searching for his dog. Plus, untangling the leash gave him something to do besides face Gianna and her inevitable questions.

But he soon realized that untangling them was awkward to say the least. There was a lot of, *Sorry. Excuse me. Watch out.* Heat rushed to his face. He wasn't sure about Gianna's reaction because he hadn't worked up the nerve to look her in the face.

That kiss had been a mistake. But it had been the most tantalizing mistake. And it hadn't done what he'd hoped it would do—get her out of his system. Instead, he wanted her now more than ever. What had he done?

CHAPTER NINE

THIS WAS GOING to be a good day.

Gianna smiled and stretched. As she tossed back the sheet, she realized it'd been a long time since she woke up with a smile on her face. And it felt good.

Only now was she able to acknowledge how unhappy she'd been while seeing Naldo. In the past, she'd always made excuses for her unhappiness. Was it possible that she'd known all along that her relationship with Naldo wasn't what it should be? Was she so eager to prove to herself and others that she could keep a man in her life that she'd blinded herself to what was in front of her face?

And what about Dario? What was up with him kissing her? Not to mention her kissing him back.

She would never admit that when he'd kissed her it was like she was floating above the earth. Or how she'd replayed that kiss over and over in her mind. No, she couldn't admit any of that because it had been a mistake. Just like all the other relationships in her life. The only person she could count on was herself. And she'd do well to remember that going forward.

She sat up and threw her legs over the edge of the bed. The best thing she could do for herself was focus on her photography. As much as she loved motion pictures, there was something about catching that special singular moment on film. And that's what she planned to do today.

She headed for the shower. It didn't take her long to rush through her morning routine, especially since she wasn't doing anything special with her hair. Once her bangs were styled, she threw the rest of her still damp hair up in a messy bun. It wasn't like anyone would notice, considering she planned to spend the day in her office.

In the kitchen, she was greeted by Tito. She knelt down and fussed over him. "Good morning." She glanced around, finding they were alone. "You know, I should be mad at you." The pup looked at her with those big innocent eyes. "Don't give me that. You know what you did—"

Woof. Woof-woof.

She loved how Tito always acted as though he knew what she was saying. He didn't understand her, did he? She shrugged. It was more fun to pretend as though he could talk back to her.

"I see how it is. You're going to act all innocent." The dog cocked his head to the side as she continued to talk. "You wrapped us up in your leash on purpose. But it isn't going to work. Dario isn't any more into me than I am into him."

Woof!

"So if you promise not to do it again, I guess I'll let it slide this time." She held her hand out to him. "Let's shake on it."

Tito hesitated and she was starting to think he didn't understand what she wanted him to do. Then the pup placed his paw in her hand and they shook.

"Very well, then." She straightened. "Looks like you're on your own this morning. Are you hungry?"

Woof.

"How did I already know that answer?" Still, she glanced around for Dario but he was nowhere to be seen. She reached for some dog treats she'd picked up in the village the prior evening.

"Don't tell your dad I gave you these."

Tito munched them down, and then without a sound, he turned and went to lie down in the open doorway.

Gianna yawned. She'd finished reading Dario's book somewhere in the wee hours of the morning. Part of her was anxious to let him know her thoughts, but the other part of her was hesitant. She knew he was really nervous about the book and she didn't know how he'd take some of what she had to say.

Still, she'd promised to tell him what she

thought and she couldn't very well back out now. He'd read something negative into her unwillingness to discuss the book. She'd just have to say what she had on her mind and hope he found it helpful.

She opened the fridge, searching for a meal they could share. She grabbed some meat, cheese, bread and fruit. In no time, she had a light brunch put together. A friendly way to lead into their serious conversation.

Balancing the tray in one hand, she moved to the patio. Dario was already seated at the table. He was hunched over his laptop. His fingers were tap-tap-tapping on the keyboard. She wanted to know what he was writing but she didn't dare disturb him.

Maybe he figured out how to fix the story and she could just keep her thoughts to herself. Could she be that lucky? She already knew the answer to that question. Luck was not on her side. Not when it came to men.

As though he could sense her standing there, looking at him, Dario's fingers paused and hovered over the keyboard. He turned his head and his gaze met hers. She couldn't tell what he was thinking because it was though a wall had gone up between them, blocking her out.

It was the kiss—it'd made a mess of things. Why hadn't she turned away? She knew why but she refused to let her thoughts go there.

"Let me just finish typing this sentence—" he glanced back down at his laptop "—and I'll get out of your way."

"There's no need to leave." She moved to the table and placed her tray in the middle. "I made enough to share."

His head lifted. Surprise flashed in his eyes. "You did?"

"Unless you'd rather be alone so you can continue working. If so, I can eat inside."

He pressed a few keys and then closed his laptop. "Don't go. After all, this is your place."

She wasn't sure how to take that. Did he want her to stay? Or was he just being polite? It was so hard to tell. And this was another reason that kiss shouldn't have happened. Now she was nervous around him. She had no idea what to say or do. And so she stood there next to the chair, unsure if she should pick up the tray and move on or if she should sit down and join him.

Deciding he was there first, and it would be best if she just moved on, she reached for the tray. At the same time, Dario stood with his laptop in hand. When she straightened, their gazes met. Heat rushed to her cheeks.

His gaze immediately dipped to the food. "We both don't have to leave. You should stay and enjoy the beautiful day. And that food looks really good."

"We...we could both stay." Her insides shivered with nerves as she waited for him to reject her offer. "There's plenty of food to share."

He didn't say anything at first. But then his gaze once again met hers and a hint of a smile pulled at his lips. "That sounds like a good idea. Thank you."

And so they both took a seat. This was awkward, even more so than their first meeting. And that was saying a lot. She had to say something, anything to ease the tension.

"About yesterday..." they said in unison.

They both grew quiet. Their gazes met and held a little longer than was necessary, but just long enough to set Gianna's heart racing. She licked her dry lips.

"I..." They both spoke again. This was getting ridiculous.

She pressed her lips together. Was he trying to say the same thing as her? That yesterday was a mistake?

"Go ahead," he said, "please say what's on your mind."

By now, her palms were damp and her mouth was dry. Why was this so difficult? After all, it wasn't like they'd spent the night together and woke up in the morning regretting their impulsive actions.

It had just been one simple kiss. Okay, maybe it hadn't exactly been simple. There may have been some steam included. Okay a lot of steam and pent-up desires.

And no, technically, it hadn't been their first kiss. There had been that kiss in front of her cousin and his brother. But it wasn't like either of them intended there to be a third kiss. That was quite out of the question.

His gaze prompted her to speak. She swallowed hard and hoped with all her might that when she spoke her voice didn't betray her nervousness. "I just wanted to say that yesterday shouldn't have happened." She glanced over at him, hoping he'd help her out. "It…it was an accident."

His brows rose high on his forehead. "It was an accident that our lips landed on each other?"

"No. I mean…uh, you know what I mean."

"Actually, I don't know."

She huffed. "It was an accident with the leash. Neither one of us was, you know, paying attention."

Was that amusement twinkling in his eyes? "And that's when your lips accidentally landed on mine?"

"No!" Heat gathered in her chest, rushed up her neck and set her whole face aflame. "I… I mean yes."

Now he outwardly smiled at her as he leaned back in his chair, enjoying her discomfort. He crossed his arms and studied her. "So which is it? Yes? Or no?"

"Stop it. You know that kiss shouldn't have happened. It was a mistake."

"So now it's a mistake, not an accident?" His smile broadened.

She glared at him. What did he find so amusing about this conversation? "Dario, stop. This isn't funny."

He sobered up enough to subdue his smile. "It's okay. We can pretend you didn't kiss me."

"What?" Surely, she hadn't heard him clearly. "I did not. You kissed me."

"Did I?" He arched his brows. "I guess if that's how you want to remember it—"

"I don't want to remember it! At. All." She jumped to her feet. She was done amusing him. "If you aren't going to take this seriously, I'm leaving."

She'd just turned to walk away when he said, "Gianna, wait."

She paused but she didn't turn around. She wasn't going to say another word because she knew he was going to turn it around on her.

"Please come back to the table."

She still didn't move, except to cross her arms. And she'd just started to think he was different than the other men who'd passed through her life. "I think it's best we stay away from each other."

A chair scraped over the patio tiles. The sound

of footsteps grew closer. She wanted to walk away before he reached her, but her pride kept her standing in the same spot.

When he came to a stop in front of her, there was no hint of amusement in his eyes. "Gianna, I'm sorry. I shouldn't have given you a hard time."

"Then why did you?"

"I don't know." He raked his fingers through his hair. "I guess I was nervous about what happened. I didn't know what to say to you."

She frowned at him. "And so you thought you'd turn it all around on me and make it seem like the kiss was all my idea?"

He shrugged. "I didn't really think about what I was saying. I was just trying to lighten the mood. I guess I failed."

"You guess you failed?"

"Okay. I did fail." He got that sheepish look on his face similar to Tito's pouty look. "I'm sorry."

"About?" She wasn't letting him off the hook that easily.

"About giving you a hard time. About not apologizing sooner. About kissing you."

"So you admit it?"

"Didn't you just hear me?"

"I mean that you kissed me." Her gaze met and held his. She ignored the way it made her heart kick up its thump-thumping.

"How about we agree that we kissed each other?" His gaze searched hers.

She'd spent all night thinking that he'd kissed her. Was it possible she might have leaned into him? Had they met in the middle?

And quite honestly, did it even matter? He was willing to meet her halfway now. But could they move beyond it? She wanted to believe they could.

She nodded. "Agreed. Can we also agree to forget it happened and never discuss it again?"

"Sounds like a plan." He sent her a hesitant smile. "Now how about we eat some of the delicious food you prepared?"

She'd totally forgotten about the meal. "Um, sure. That sounds good."

Woof. Woof.

Dario ran a hand over Tito's head. "What are you so excited for? Do you think we're going to share the food with you?"

Woof. Woof.

"Don't let him fool you," she said. "He already begged me for a treat."

Dario turned back to the dog. "Is that true?"

Tito whined as though he were trying to speak.

Gianna couldn't help but smile. As she did, she realized the tension that had been crackling in the air had lifted. Their relationship was different since the kiss, but if they both tried, the rest of their time together didn't have to be painfully awkward.

At least they no longer had to pretend they were in love. She was certain that playing lovers was what had prompted that kiss. Yes, that was definitely it. Thankfully, they were back to being just friends. Nothing more.

CHAPTER TEN

HE DREADED WHAT was coming next. The discussion about his book. If she loved it, wouldn't she have said something by now?

Dario popped a grape in his mouth. He hadn't eaten much. As hard as he'd tried to put Gianna at ease about the kiss, he was still hung up on it.

He'd kissed many women in his lifetime but none of them had rocked his world like Gianna had done. But he didn't do relationships. He couldn't let himself count on someone else for his happiness, the way his mother did—man after man.

But now, as they finished eating, Dario needed to think of anything but that kiss. He chanced a glance Gianna's way as she took a sip of fresh squeezed lemonade. What did she think of his book? The question hovered on the tip of his tongue. He held back. What if she hated it? Or what if she liked it but was upset with him for hassling her about the kiss and said she didn't like it out of spite?

He halted his nervous thoughts. He knew Gianna well enough to know she wasn't a spiteful person. She was kind and caring. She went out of her way for people—especially him. So why was he hesitating?

"I finished reading your book," Gianna said, as though she'd been reading his thoughts.

He swallowed hard. "You did?"

She nodded. "That's why I slept in again this morning."

He tried to read her face to figure out whether she'd liked the book or not. But her expression wasn't giving anything away. "And what did you think?"

"I didn't want to put it down."

He smiled. "So you agree with me that it doesn't need anything else and I should submit it to my editor as is?"

She didn't say anything for a moment. The longer she was quiet, the more he lost hope that he'd nailed the book.

"Gianna?"

"I love your writing. You have a way with descriptions. They're so vivid."

He appreciated her compliment but he knew she was avoiding the main issue. "But is there something important missing from the book?"

She drew in a visible breath. Her gaze avoided his. "I'm not an editor or agent. My opinion shouldn't matter."

He knew she was skirting the answer. "Gianna, please, just say it."

Her gaze met his. Sympathy emanated from her eyes. "I just didn't feel the same growth in the hero as I did in the first book."

It was more definitive than what his agent had given him. But he just didn't get it. "It's not the same," he said. "Ator isn't going to grow the way he did in the first book. He was just a child in the beginning of that book and he grew through the chapters, coming into his legacy as leader of the Lavar."

"I understand that. But there's still something missing—"

"There's a lot to the book. There's a new threat to the Lavarians. And there's a threat within his own ranks."

"I know and that part is really good." She hesitated, as though she were going to say more but then changed her mind.

It was hard hearing that other people didn't see his book the way he did. There was a point where he hadn't thought he'd ever finish the book and the fact he had, well, it was a major miracle. Then he'd gone over it and over it, layering in emotions and descriptions. He'd poured hundreds of hours into that manuscript.

He just didn't think he had anything else to add. There were a ton of action scenes. There were victories and some defeats for the hero.

There was uncertainty of whether he would or wouldn't succeed in his mission. What else could the book need?

"What if you had something about his personal life in there?" she asked.

"It's all personal to him. Ator's whole life is on the line." Dario knew he was being contrary. He didn't mean to be, but if he didn't defend his book, who would?

Still, there was that little voice in the back of his head that warned he might very well be missing something important. What if he was too stubborn to see his book's imperfections? He wanted his book to be the very best it could be.

It was about far more than the money he would receive if the publisher accepted the book. After all, he was a Marchello—he had a trust fund that he couldn't spend in a lifetime. His connection to this book went so much deeper. He could envision the scenes in his mind. He'd really connected with the characters and he wanted to share them with his readers.

But according to his agent and now Gianna, he hadn't dug deep enough into the hero. That hurt because he'd thought he'd done a really good job with Ator. But he knew if it wasn't good enough, the editor might not even bother to give him revisions. He might just outright reject the manuscript and ask for the advance back. In the publishing world, there were no guarantees.

"Okay." He couldn't believe what he was about to say. "Tell me what you think is missing."

"I told you, I'm no literary professional."

"True. But you're a reader. And you said you really liked the first book, so I trust you."

"I loved the first book. And I think this book could be even better."

"If I wrote what?"

She shrugged. "Ator needs someone close to him."

"He has his best friend, who leads up the strike team."

"Yes, but his best friend answers to him. And when it comes down to it, he backs off when they argue, as you would expect. He needs someone he has no control over. Someone who isn't afraid to speak their mind."

"Someone like you?"

"Someone like me?" She shook her head. "You're joking right?"

Was he? He wasn't even sure why he'd said it. "Well, you aren't afraid to speak your mind. You're willing to tell me what you think without backing down."

"Am I that bad?"

"No. That isn't what I mean." He paused to give her idea some thought. Maybe she was onto something. Because there was definitely something in the heated wordplay between them earlier and maybe a little sexual tension—okay a lot of the latter. Not that he would admit it to her or anyone else.

"What are you thinking?" Her voice interrupted his thoughts.

The truth was he didn't like where his thoughts were going. Not at all. Because thinking about his attraction to Gianna would only make their current arrangement more complicated.

He shook his head, chasing the thought from his mind. "Nothing. It won't work."

"What won't work? Giving him a girlfriend?"

His jaw tightened. "I don't write romance. No way. I'm not doing it."

Gianna planted her hands on her hips as her fine brows drew together into a firm line. "What exactly are you saying?"

"That I don't write that sappy, emotional stuff."

Her mouth gaped.

"Why are you looking at me like that? That romance stuff is for women. I write fantasy and action."

"You mean all that macho stuff?"

He shrugged again. "Guys don't want to read all that mushy stuff."

"Really? Are you sure?"

He frowned at her. He didn't want to write about matters of the heart. It was way outside his wheelhouse. "I'm not doing it."

She shrugged. "Okay." There was a tone to her voice he couldn't quite place, like she thought he was making a big mistake. "It was just a suggestion."

"That stuff is okay for other people to write but not me."

"You mean, it's okay for women to write romance but not a big tough guy like you."

"No." He raked his fingers through his hair. "That isn't what I mean."

"Oh, wait. Are you saying you don't believe in love?"

This time he was the one who shrugged and looked away. "Something like that." When she didn't say anything, he chanced a glance her way. "What?"

"Nothing."

"Oh, you're thinking something. Just say it."

Gianna shook her head. When her gaze met his, there was sympathy radiating from her eyes. "I shouldn't have pushed so hard. I'm sorry—"

"Don't."

"Don't, what?" The sympathy was still there in her eyes. "I'm just trying to apologize."

"No. You feel sorry for me. And I don't want your sympathy. I don't need it." Why did she think because he didn't believe in love that he should be pitied? He was fine without it. He didn't need it.

"You know, I understand what it's like to get your heart broken. I'm sorry it happened to you too."

He held up his palms. "Whoa! You have this all wrong. No one hurt me." It wasn't exactly true. "No one had to hurt me for me not to believe in true love."

Her gaze narrowed in on him. "So you truly believe that two people can't live happily-ever-after?"

"That's a fairy tale. And fairy tales aren't true." She frowned as she considered his answer. He cleared his throat. "You disagree?"

"Actually, I was wondering if that was my problem. Maybe I've been wanting the illusion of something that doesn't exist outside of books and movies."

He'd never gotten this response before. Any time he'd mentioned his disbelief in true love, he'd always come up against strong opposition. But Gianna was different. A smile tugged at the corner of his lips. Then he noticed the shattered and disillusioned look in Gianna's eyes. She wanted true love to exist, which quite frankly surprised him after her last disastrous relationship.

He tilted his head ever so slightly to the side as he continued to study her. "You seem disappointed to think that true love might not exist. Why?" When her eyes widened with confusion, he further explained his train of thought. "I mean, you've had some bad luck where love is concerned, and yet, you still seem to want to know that it's out there. Why would you want to risk being hurt again?"

"Why wouldn't I?"

"I don't know. That's what I'm asking you."

She frowned at him. "Wait. You're serious. You've really never been in love?"

He shook his head and glanced away. He didn't deserve or need her feeling sorry for him. Was it so hard to believe he was fine on his own? Needing someone was a weakness. His mother had that weakness, moving from man to man to man. He wouldn't be weak like her. He just wouldn't.

Gianna's inquisitive stare searched him for answers. He didn't owe her any explanations. There was absolutely no reason to drag his messy family history into this conversation. Why did everyone seem to think it was strange that he didn't believe in fantasies? Like someone was really going to stick with him through thick and thin. He might write fantasies but he didn't believe they'd come true.

When things got tough, the door was the way to go. It's what his father did when Dario was young. Apparently, a family of four was more than his father was willing to deal with. And after he was gone, everything else just fell apart. Love wasn't worth all that pain—not when it didn't last.

When he glanced back at Gianna, she was still staring at him as though trying to dissect what had happened to him to stop him from believing in true love. "Stop it."

"Stop, what?"

"Looking at me like…like I'm broken. I'm not."

Her eyes widened. "You think you're broken?"

"I didn't say that. I mean, I did…" He rubbed the tense muscles in the back of his neck and groaned in frustration. "I don't want to discuss this anymore."

Buzz. Buzz.

He welcomed the interruption and withdrew his phone from his pocket. "It's my grandmother. She rarely calls me. I should get it."

Gianna nodded just as her phone went off. She checked the caller ID: Vera Cappellini. "It's my mother."

He had a feeling their simultaneous calls weren't a coincidence. He moved toward the other side of the patio to give Gianna some privacy.

"Nonna, what's wrong?"

"Is that any way to greet your grandmother?"

"I'm sorry. I'm just not used to you calling me." He sensed she had something important on her mind and was just working up to saying it. "What did you want to discuss?"

"I thought perhaps you had something to tell me."

A cold sense of dread came over him. He

should have known his brother wouldn't keep news of his engagement to himself.

Dario swallowed hard. "Regarding what?"

His grandmother sighed. "I heard you got engaged. I thought I'd hear news like that directly from you."

Dario's gaze immediately sought out Gianna. As she talked, she waved her hand about. She only did that when she was worked up.

He overheard her say, "I'm sorry, Mamma. I should have called you right away." She paused and then said, "Yes, I'm engaged."

"Dario, are you still there?" His grandmother's voice drew back his attention.

"Yes, Nonna. I'm here."

Thanks to his brother and her cousin, their secret engagement wasn't so secret any longer. This wasn't good. Not good at all.

It was as if his life kept getting increasingly intertwined with Gianna's. Before his grandmother hung up, she made sure he knew to bring Gianna to their anniversary weekend—because a single dinner just wasn't enough. And they were just dying to meet his fiancée...

CHAPTER ELEVEN

HER WORLD FELT as though it were spinning off its axis.

Gianna felt bad about letting her mouth run amuck yesterday while talking to Dario. She'd only meant to help with the book and somehow it had spun out of control. She didn't care what he said—someone had hurt him deeply and left painful scars. Her heart ached for him.

She'd always known love growing up. In fact, she sometimes thought her parents had loved her too much. It was part of the reason she'd decided to move to Lake Como. She needed some distance from her parents in order to make her own mistakes without them interfering, in their well-meaning ways, and trying to fix everything for her.

She didn't like to make mistakes—in fact, they were downright awful—but she liked to think she'd learned from each of hers. Perhaps she still had a lot of learning to do.

The second thing to go wrong yesterday was

finding out that her parents knew she was engaged. Her mother had been so happy and that made Gianna feel that much worse. Still, she'd made a promise to Dario. And as far as her parents were concerned, the damage was done. Even her father was excited. They were anxious to meet her fiancé.

After both Dario and Gianna had finished speaking with their respective families, neither had been in the mood to speak to the other. Their little fib had taken wings and grown. Now it felt as though everyone knew—everyone that mattered. They'd each gone their separate ways to deal with their guilt in their own way.

She'd decided one thing last night. Though she still believed in true love, she wasn't so sure it was for everyone. She'd also realized that you can't create it just because it's what you thought you wanted—as she'd learned the hard way—and if it came, it would come in its own time.

She needed to make things right with Dario. She made her way out to the patio area, fully expecting him to be seated at the table with his fingers moving rapidly over the keyboard while Tito laid by his side, but he wasn't there.

Her gaze moved to the French doors of the guesthouse. She was surprised to find them closed. Usually they were wide open, letting the gentle breeze rush through, just like she did with the doors of the main house. Was it possible he'd kept them closed because he was mad at her?

No. Surely not. Yes, she'd pushed him about putting some romance into his book and perhaps she'd taken it too far when she'd made it personal, but was he really going to avoid her for the rest of the month?

She moved across the patio and rapped her knuckles on the door. "Dario? Are you in there?"

Woof! Woof-woof!

Well, Tito was definitely in there. And she knew Dario didn't like to go anywhere without him. Actually, they were rather cute together. Dario might think he was immune to love, but she'd seen the way he looked at his dog and there was a deep and abiding love between them. So what if it wasn't a romantic love. The way she saw it, if he was capable of caring that much for an animal, he could also care deeply for a human—if he'd just let himself. Not that she was applying for the position or anything. It was merely an observation.

The door swung open. Dario stood there with his hair going every direction, which she'd come to learn was what happened when he was hard at work. His eyes were a bit bloodshot with shadows beneath them. And his clothes, well, they were the same ones he'd had on yesterday. Was it more than writing that had him looking so disheveled?

"Dario, are you all right?"

He seemed distracted, as though he were lost in his thoughts. "What?"

"I asked if you're feeling all right."

"I'm fine. Did you need something? Because I have to be going."

"No. Not really." She should apologize for pushing him yesterday, but she struggled for the right words. "I, uh…"

"Okay, then. I'll talk to you later." And with that, the door closed.

What in the world had just happened? Her lips pressed into a firm line that slowly sunk down into a frown. That had not gone at all like she'd planned.

Her stubborn streak kicked in. Who was he to shut the door in her face? She wasn't walking away until she'd said what she'd walked over here to say.

She tightened her hand and knocked firmly on the door again. This time she didn't call out. She knew he was in there and he knew she was waiting to speak to him.

It took a minute. A very long minute. Then the door swung open. His handsome face was marred with frown lines. So he wasn't happy to see her again. So be it.

"This won't take long," she said.

"That's good. I need to get back."

To what? His dog? The television? What was it that had him so distracted? And then she thought of his book and the revisions. Could that be what had him so distracted? The thought lightened her mood.

"I just came to say that I'm sorry I pushed you so hard about…" Her voice trailed off as suddenly she felt very uncomfortable about bringing up the *L* word with him. Yesterday, it had just rolled out as a part of a bigger conversation. Today, however, there was no conversation. In fact, Dario kept his hand on the door as though he couldn't wait to shut it. "Anyway, I'm sorry if things were said that shouldn't have been."

He shrugged. "It's fine. Is that all?"

Really? That's all he was going to say? She was beginning to dislike the word *fine*. Well, if he didn't want to talk to her, then she had other things to do.

"Yes, that's all." She turned and walked away.

The door closed behind her.

She had to admit, if only to herself, that her pride was stung. Something had shifted between them after those heart-pounding, toe-curling kisses. She wasn't going to fool herself into thinking they were in love. Been there. Done that. This thing with Dario felt so different from anything she'd ever experienced.

But somewhere along the way she'd thought that they'd formed a solid friendship. After all, she'd told him more about her current life than her cousin—her best friend. And yet, it all came to an abrupt end when she'd challenged his disbelief in true love.

She grabbed her backpack and slung her camera around her neck. She was off. And she didn't know when she'd be back. Not that Dario would miss her or anything.

His fingers pounded on the keyboard.

His thoughts came so rapidly that his fingers couldn't keep up.

Dario didn't know how many hours he'd been sitting with his laptop in hand. His fingers ached from the lengthy typing. His neck was stiff from leaning over his screen. Every other muscle protested from his lack of movement. And yet, he continued to write.

He'd started in bed when he couldn't sleep. He'd made notes and written down random thoughts of how a romance thread could play a part in the book.

At first, he didn't want it to play a very big part. After all, this was a fantasy/action book. It wasn't some heartfelt, tearful paperback. He didn't want to lose the oomph! And he had to stay true to his hero's macho attitude. But maybe, just maybe, there was a way to add the element. It would make everyone happy. He hoped.

In his mind, he played out scenario after scenario, but none felt right. His hero, Ator, didn't believe he deserved a personal life. His life was dedicated to the preservation of the civilization of Lavar. So that meant whomever Ator got involved with, it would be such a fierce love that even the hero would not be able to ignore it.

As Dario thought about this romance, he noticed how his thoughts kept slipping back to Gianna. She was a force unlike any other he'd ever known. While other women were more inclined to be agreeable with him—well, as long as they thought they had a chance to snare one of the rich and eligible Marchello brothers—Gianna didn't care about impressing him. She spoke her mind. And that impressed him. His hero needed a heroine like Gianna—up front and in his face when she thought he was messing things up.

At first, Dario tried using one of Ator's household staff for a love interest, but it didn't take him long to realize she was no match for the hero. The ideal woman needed to be the hero's equal. Just as Gianna was his equal in smarts and matters of the heart. She might talk a big game about true love, but he knew she was just as leery of it as he was.

And so he kept writing. Note after note. Thought after thought. Never deleting anything because he never knew what idea he might need in the future.

He couldn't let himself get distracted with phone calls, emails or even his gorgeous housemate. If he lost his train of thought, he feared it wouldn't come back.

It had happened to him before. He'd be onto a new thread in a book and the phone would ring. By the time he got off the phone, he'd lost his rhythm. Trying to climb back inside the thoughts of a character was not as easy as it seemed. Sometimes the hero's thoughts flowed and other times it was a process of pulling out one word at a time at a snail's pace.

Because at last he had it—the perfect subplot. The heroine's name was Sefinna, a high-ranking soldier in the enemy forces.

The first time they meet, it's in battle. Instead of killing her, he spares her life. Her culture says that she now owes him her life—but not her army's secrets.

Like moths to a flame, they are drawn to each other. They fight their feelings—but for how long? If they were to act on their feelings and it was uncovered, it would mean the death of both of them.

Dario liked the subplot. He really did. But he also kept telling himself he would fix things with Gianna in a little bit. By the time he was ready for a break, it was late. She had probably already called it a night. He noticed she liked to go to bed early so she could rise before the sun, whereas he was more of a night owl.

But now that he'd reached a point in his writing that he was comfortable taking a break, he stepped onto the patio. He was surprised to find Gianna had just gotten out of the pool. She finished drying off and then wrapped a towel around herself. When she turned and spotted him, she jumped.

"Sorry," he said. "I didn't mean to startle you."

"Well, the pool is all yours." She started toward the main house.

"Gianna, wait." He approached her.

She stopped and turned. "It's late and I'm tired."

"This won't take long. I just want to say I'm sorry for being so abrupt earlier."

"You mean yesterday?"

Yesterday? Had it been that long ago? His sleep-deprived brain realized she must be right. "Yes. I've been working on some ideas to fix the book and I guess I got a bit obsessed."

Her gaze searched his face. "When's the last time you slept?"

"It's been a while. But I promise you when the book is sold, you'll be the first person to read it."

"Get some rest. We can talk tomorrow." She turned and went into the house.

Tito followed her. Even his dog had abandoned him. He wanted to call out to Gianna and ask her to sit with him for a while. He missed her company.

He remained quiet as he stood all alone. Being

alone was what he wanted, right? He didn't need anyone. Needing someone made you vulnerable. His mind flashed back to him as a child, watching his mother drive away, leaving him and his brother behind.

He slammed the door on the painful memory. He was okay on his own. He turned and headed for the guesthouse. If he needed company, he had the characters in his book.

CHAPTER TWELVE

THE NEXT FEW DAYS, Gianna split her time between taking photos while on nature walks and working in her office. She'd taken a lot more pictures since she'd been home than she imagined possible. But the weather was too nice to be stuck inside all day.

She thought about grabbing her camera, her tripod and going off on one of her nature walks. Her entry for the photo competition was due soon and she still didn't think she had a winner out of the hundreds of photos she'd taken so far. She pulled her latest batch of photos up on her extra-large monitor. There were some good ones, but for one reason or another, she rejected them all. None of them had what it took to stand out in the crowd.

Just then her phone rang. It was her agent. He had a lead on a new assignment for her. It was another nature show with a different host. This time she'd be in Alaska.

She knew the area was beautiful but the idea

of roughing it didn't appeal to her. At least that's what she told herself was the reason she wasn't anxious to leave Lake Como. It certainly had nothing to do with her sleep-deprived, grumpy housemate. Nothing at all.

She told her agent she'd think about it. He said she had some time. Production didn't start for a couple of months.

Maybe what she needed was a break. She headed to the kitchen to pack some food, but passing by the open doors, she noticed Dario working on the patio. His posture was rigid as he leaned over his laptop, rereading what he'd written. Then he blew out a breath and slouched back in the chair. His fingers raked through his hair. It didn't look like the writing was going well.

She thought about going out and speaking with him. Things between them had been rocky lately. She'd like to fix it. However, it needed to be more than a brief conversation. Perhaps he needed to get away from this place too—away from his computer—away from the stress of work.

A little later, Gianna emerged from the house in jean shorts, a pink blouse and one of her grandmother's hats. Her grandmother had had an obsession with hats. Once in a while, Gianna would wear one. Today, she'd chosen a big straw hat with a white bow and pink flowers. It was more than a retro fashion statement. It would help protect her from the sunshine because where they were going there wouldn't be any shade.

Dario glanced up from his laptop. "Don't you look cute?"

She smiled and curtsied. "Why thank you."

He chuckled. "You're in a good mood. I take it things are going well with your photography business?"

She shrugged. "I guess you could say that. But it's not really a business. Right now, it's more of a hobby. But my agent called with a job offer."

"Is that a good thing?"

"I don't know. It'd mean living out of a duffel bag again."

"Then turn it down."

"It's not that easy. I need money to pay the bills." Though she could honestly say she wasn't jumping at the offer. The more time she spent in Gemma, the more she wanted to stay here.

"Your photography could be a business, if you wanted."

It was though he could read her mind. "I've dreamed about opening a little shop to sell my prints, but it would take all my savings and I'm just not sure anyone would be interested in my work. After all, I'm a nobody in the photography world."

"I think you should do it, if it'll make you happy. I can guarantee you'll have one client. Me. I think you're amazingly talented."

Her face grew warm. "Thank you. But that's something to ponder another day. Right now, I have other plans."

"Are you off to take more photos?"

"Not today. I thought we'd have an outing."

"We? As in you and me?" When she nodded, he said, "Thanks. But I don't think so. I have too much work to do here."

"Really? Because it looks to me like you're stuck."

"That obvious?"

She nodded.

He frowned. "I'll get it. I… I just have to keep working on it."

She approached him. "Or maybe you need to give your mind a break."

"I don't have time for a break. My deadline for these revisions is almost here."

"All the more reason for you to relax." Sensing he was going to refuse her again, she added, "I may not be a writer, but I can't imagine you can just force your imagination to cooperate out of pure will."

"Sadly, you're right. It doesn't work that way. The harder I search for the next words, the harder they are to find."

She closed his laptop. "Come with me."

"Gianna…really I can't. You know how important this book is to me."

"I promise if you come with me now, I'll leave you alone the rest of the day."

"Where are we going?"

"To lunch." She held up her grandmother's picnic basket.

"So now you're bribing me?"

She smiled. "I don't know. Is it working?"

When he blew out a sigh, she knew she'd won. "Yes, it is. Lead the way. Come on, Tito."

Her smile faltered. "About that. I don't think Tito will appreciate this particular outing."

"He wouldn't?" Dario looked confused and a bit disappointed. "Where exactly are we going?"

"Someplace an excitable puppy shouldn't be." She turned to Tito. "I'm sorry, fella. Maybe next time."

Once Tito was situated in the guesthouse, they set off on their adventure. Gianna just hoped he liked her surprise. She'd find out soon enough.

Sailing.

Dario couldn't believe he was sitting in a rowboat of all things. He quite honestly had never gone rowing before. Sure, he'd been on luxury yachts numerous times, as well as cruise ships, but never a modest rowboat. He wasn't sure what to make of it.

His gaze moved to Gianna, who smiled as she looked out over the tranquil water. After he'd insisted on doing the rowing, Gianna used her camera to take some photos of him, of the water and of the mountains in the background. She seemed to be enjoying herself. And he had to admit the physical activity was doing him some good, as well. He didn't feel nearly as stiff and utterly stressed.

"So do you approve of your surprise?" she asked.

"I do. I've never done this before." He glanced around at the shoreline. "It gives me a whole new perspective on the area from here."

Gianna let go of her camera, letting it dangle from the strap around her neck. "Your parents didn't do things like this when you were young?"

He shook his head. "My family was very different from yours. Even from a young age, there were a lot of expectations as far as doing well in school to being at the top of sports. There wasn't much time to have fun."

"You mean your mother and father didn't let you be normal kids?"

He had opened Pandora's box and now he didn't know how to close it. And to his surprise, he wasn't even sure he wanted to close it. As he'd come to learn, Gianna was easy to talk to, and though she didn't always agree with him, she made him see things from a different perspective.

Not that he wanted to think about his dysfunctional family, but he felt as though he owed her the truth. After all, she'd agreed to portray herself as his fake fiancée when there wasn't much in it for her. Who did something like that?

A gentle breeze rushed over him, soothing his frazzled nerves. But prying open the rusty door to the past wasn't easy. He didn't talk about it. Ever. Even as a young child, he'd learned how to swiftly change the subject. These days, he had it down to a fine art.

He shook his head. "You don't want to hear about my messed-up family."

"Messed up? Does this have something to do with why you never mention your mother or father?"

He nodded.

When she spoke, her voice was soft. "Why is that?"

There was shame in his past—in the Marchellos' past—that no one in his family spoke of. Not even amongst themselves. The things he knew of his parents he'd pieced together bit by bit over the course of his lifetime.

He stared out over the water. "From what I gather, my parents were forced together."

"You mean as in an arranged marriage?"

He shook his head. "Not exactly. Their families knew each other. They moved in the same circles. There were expectations from the time they were young children. From what I gathered, they dated in school. They broke up at some point and then much later, with pressure from their families, they got back together and married."

"I feel bad for them. That's a lot of pressure to put on kids."

Dario continued. If he didn't get it out now, he wouldn't later. "Soon, my brother came along. My father was working in the family business under my grandfather's guidance, which is no easy task. Don't get me wrong, I love my grandfather. But he can be difficult. Anyway, I was born a couple of years later and apparently it was too much for their marriage. My father bailed. He up and quit his job, his family, everyone."

Dario still remembered the day. He'd been young, only five or so. But his parents had a really loud argument. His father packed a few things and was out the door. That was the day Dario's world changed forever.

"I'm so sorry you went through that, but at least you had your mother."

He shrugged off her sympathy. "She stuck it out for a year or so. By then she was divorced and on the hunt for husband number two."

"What happened to you and your brother?"

"My mother deposited us on my grandparents' doorstep. It was just supposed to be for the summer, but she never came back to take us home."

Tears started to well up in Gianna's eyes. "That's the saddest thing I think I've ever heard."

He shrugged off her sympathy. "It's fine. We're

fine." They weren't. Not really. But dwelling on it helped no one. "It's all in the past."

"Is it?" she asked. "Do you ever see your parents?"

"Over the years, they've drifted in and out of our lives. The last time I saw my mother, she was on her second or was it her third husband? It's hard to keep track."

"And your father?"

"He's pretty much a nomad, moving from place to place. He never remarried. I think he had enough of it the first time around."

"At least you have your grandparents."

"True. But they are cool and distant from each other. They don't argue, at least not in front of my brother and me, but they've never been affectionate in front of us either."

"Oh. No wonder you don't believe in love."

Dario gripped the oars and resumed rowing. He needed something to do to avoid seeing the sympathy in her eyes. It made him feel like that small helpless child once more—it was a feeling he never wanted to experience again.

"My grandparents raised my brother and me. Franco was always anxious to join the family business. It was dictated that I would join him at the helm when the time came. The only problem was that no one asked me if it's what I wanted.

"I went to college and when I graduated, I

worked my way up through the business like my father and brother had done. I'm good at what I do. The only problem is I don't like it. I wish I did. I feel guilty for rejecting what my family has built up over generations."

"You shouldn't feel guilty. You can't control where your interests lie. If you feel guilty, then I'll have to feel guilty about not staying and helping with my parents' market or marrying someone who would one day take it over."

His gaze met hers. "Sounds like we're in the same boat."

"Literally." She smiled at her joke.

He smiled too. It was nice to know that finally someone understood him. Once, he'd tried to talk to his brother about their parents. Franco said he understood what he was feeling, but Dario knew his business-driven brother never really understood.

Dario paused the rowing. "I've been a reader all my life. It's what got me through the breakup of my family and everything else. The older I got, the more I read until I had a library of paperbacks. Fantasy books were always my favorite."

"I like to read romance, but I think you already figured that out."

He nodded. "I noticed them on the bookcases in the living room."

"So how did you get started writing?"

He shook his head. "That part's really boring."

"No, it isn't." She looked at him expectantly. "I'd love to hear it, if you're willing to share."

"One evening, I came home from work and I decided to try and write a book. I'd taken creative writing in college but that was a lot different than writing a complete book. My first attempt was a disaster. So I delved deeper into the writing world. To my surprise, there really is a world of writers who live online. Though the writer's world spans the globe, thanks to the internet, it's actually a pretty small community."

"It seems like you can find most anything on the internet these days. I just joined a group of photographers. They talk about all the new equipment out there and how it compares to the older stuff. I listen but I haven't ventured into any of the discussions."

"I understand. It took me a while to speak up. An online acquaintance guided me to online classes for writers. Little by little, I figured out where I'd gone wrong. It took a long time for me to finish writing my first book as my work in the family business includes a lot of overtime and business dinners. I still have that story somewhere on my laptop."

"That's exciting. You could publish it too."

He shook his head. "I don't think so. I made a lot of mistakes with it. *The Rise of Lavar* is my second book.

"It took me almost two years until I finished

it. I was certain it was going to be a best seller. It was so much better than my first attempt. After all, I'd poured my heart and soul into it. I sent it off to an agent. The agent replied immediately with good news and bad news. First, they liked my voice. But second, the book was much too long with way too much description. So I started making the story a lot leaner. It's harder figuring out what to cut than it sounds. I sent the revised manuscript back to the agent. He passed. The next agent passed. And so it went, agent after agent. I was just about to give up when an agent finally took an interest in my book. It took a while to find the right publisher and well, you know the rest of it."

"Yes, I do. Now I can say I knew you when."

He laughed out loud. "You make it sound like I'll be famous."

"You are famous."

"No, I'm not." He didn't feel famous, even though his book had sold close to a million copies around the world and there was even a fan club started online. "I'm just me."

"You can't ever give up on your dream."

This was his chance to speak up and help her. "I won't give up on my dream, if you won't give up on yours."

"What dream is that?"

"I see you with your camera. You're rarely

without it. I wouldn't be surprised if you sleep with it—"

"I'm not that bad…am I?"

He smiled and nodded. "I see the way your face lights up when you find something to photograph. It makes you happy."

"Working on a film crew makes me happy too."

"Does it really? Do you get out of bed before the sun so you can shoot the sunrise?"

"I do…but only because my alarm goes off and I know if I'm not where I'm supposed to be on time that a lot of people are going to get upset with me."

"See. I was right. It's not the same."

She sighed. "Okay. You're right. I like photography better. But I don't know if I can make a living doing it."

"You won't know unless you try." He glanced down at the picnic basket. "Now how about we eat? I'm starved."

He'd never been so close to a person. Gianna didn't reject him because of his dysfunctional family or call him crazy because he didn't want to be a part of his family's successful business and bring home an enormous paycheck. She liked him just the way he was without wanting him to change.

He'd kiss her right now if he thought he could pull it off without tipping over the boat. The idea teased and tempted him. What was life without a few risks? He let go of the oars and went to stand—the boat tilted to the side.

"What are you doing?" Gianna frowned at him. "Stop moving."

He settled back on the seat. "Sorry. I was going to, um…help with lunch."

"I've got it. Sit still. My idea of fun isn't swimming to shore."

And so the moment had passed. He'd missed the perfect moment to feel her lips beneath his. He knew it was for the best, even if it didn't feel like it. After all, relationships didn't work out. But Gianna was making him wish they could be the exception.

CHAPTER THIRTEEN

THE LITTLE WHITE cursor hovered over the send button.

Days had passed in a coffee-driven blur. One day had turned into two. And before he knew it, nearly two weeks had flown by. He'd never written with such passion. Gianna had made sure he stopped to eat, but otherwise she'd given him the space to finish the revisions.

And now the moment of truth was upon him. He'd completed the book almost a week early. It was all thanks to Gianna and her constant encouragement. No matter what, she continued to believe in him.

The cursor continued to hover over the send button. Why was he hesitating? He'd done his best work. Hadn't he?

His heart raced as doubt crept into his thoughts. Mentally, he went over his manuscript one last time. Was the new story thread carried through the entire story? Yes. Had he left any plot threads dangling? He didn't think so. But with one hundred and fifty thousand words, it was easy to miss something.

In the next thought, he realized he was overthinking things. After all, this wasn't the final draft of the book—far from it. He still had time to fix anything he'd missed. Plus there would be a number of eyes that read over it before it went to press—well, that's if it went to press. He sure hoped it would, but there were no guarantees.

He'd read on an online forum how the book market could change suddenly. What was hot one day wasn't hot the next day. In the past year, since his first book was released, had the wave of reader excitement for his characters passed him by? He sure hoped not.

Was there anything else he could add to the book at this point to make it better? He didn't think so. So there was nothing else to do... He pressed Send.

Euphoria rushed through his system. At this particular moment, he didn't care if anyone liked it or not. The point was that he'd finished the second book in the series. It had a beginning, a middle and an end. What more could anyone ask for?

Then again, there was one more thing.

He'd come up with the best hook for the end of the book. When Ator and Sefinna give in to their desires, there's a creek of a floorboard outside the door. Has their secret been found out? Will they pay the ultimate price for their love?

He smiled. Readers would have to stay tuned for the next book. At this point, he had no idea where they went from there. He'd figure it out another day.

Needing someone to celebrate with him, he glanced over at Tito, who had dragged his dog bed out onto the patio. He was now stretched out in it, sleeping.

"Hey, boy, guess what?"

Tito pried one eye open.

"I finished my book. Isn't that great?"

He didn't get so much as a wag of the dog's tail. Tito closed his eye, yawned and rolled over. So much for being his man's best friend.

Dario's thoughts turned to Gianna. Without her, none of this would have happened. Tonight, they were going to live it up. After all, she'd put up with him living much like a zombie these past few weeks.

He closed his laptop and jumped up from the patio table. "Gianna!" He started toward the main house. Where was she? He didn't recall her leaving, but he realized that sometimes he got lost in his thoughts and missed what was right in front of him.

"Gianna? Are you here?"

"In here," she called from the back of her house.

He followed her voice to the room that she'd converted into her office. Her desk faced the window so she could look out over the lush hillside. He couldn't blame her. It was an amazing view. But her back was to him so he wasn't able to read her expression.

"Hey, are you busy?" He really hoped she'd say she wasn't.

"I am. What do you need?"

It wasn't fair for him to drag her away from her work just because he'd finished his own. After all, she'd given him plenty of room while he'd finished his book.

"Ah…" He hesitated. "It's nothing. I'll talk to you later." A bit deflated, he turned and walked away.

Gianna being busy shouldn't douse his mood. He'd accomplished something big—something he hadn't been sure he'd be able to do. But celebrating alone didn't appeal to him. He could walk into the village. There would be plenty of people there, but the thought of celebrating with a bunch of strangers didn't appeal to him either.

There was only one person he wanted to celebrate with—Gianna. He noticed as more and more time passed that he really looked forward to spending time with her. There was something special about her—something down-to-earth.

When she was upset with him, it showed. When she wanted to have a good time, it wasn't to get all dressed up and go into the city to be seen. Instead, Gianna liked to watch a movie or take a walk in nature. She was so very different from the women he dated. And yet, when she did have to go out and be seen, she knew how to dress up and present herself as if she were a movie star.

But a little voice inside him said that this was nothing more than an infatuation. True love did not exist. All he had to do was look at his grandparents and parents. His grandparents tolerated each other but he never saw any real affection between them. And then his parents, well, they were the very definition of dysfunctional. So much so that not only did their marriage fail but they were also barely present in either of their sons' lives.

He didn't want a loveless marriage. The thought of barely speaking to Gianna and merely passing her in the hallway made him sad. Or worse, fighting with her daily like his parents had done would be agony.

It was best to keep his distance from relationships. It'd worked for him so far. But he knew Gianna had somehow breached the walls he'd put up around his heart. He felt something for her—something he'd never felt for anyone else. But he wasn't ready or willing to examine those emotions too closely.

"Dario, sorry about that. I was in the middle of uploading some photos to a website." Gianna strolled out to the patio. "What did you need?"

ou like being engaged to me? I mean, I know hat a catch I am." He sent her a teasing smile, ut there was a part of him that was serious.

"Don't you wish—" she said quickly. "No. t's just that I worry about ruining this event for hem."

"You think they'll be upset by the current status of my love life?"

She shrugged. "I don't know them but you do. Do they worry about you?"

For the longest time, he thought his grandparents were only worried about his future in the family business. But he'd noticed how excited his grandmother had become upon the news of his engagement. She was even talking about wedding plans. At the time, the thought of walking down the aisle had sent cold chills down his spine, but now it wasn't sounding nearly as intimidating...so long as it was Gianna by his side. The thought startled him. Were his thoughts being influenced by more than just his writing?

"Well, my grandmother was excited to meet your family at the party and start the wedding plans."

"My family! She contacted them?"

"It appears my brother gave my grandmother Carla's contact information and from there she was able to reach your parents. She personally invited them. I thought you knew."

"No, I didn't know." She frowned. "Now we

"I hit Send."

Her eyes widened. "On your book?"

His mood lifted and he smiled. "Yes. It's finally gone."

"That's awesome." She rushed over to him. At first, he wasn't sure what she was planning to do but then she threw her arms around him and hugged him tight. "I'm so proud of you."

His arms snaked their way around her slender waist. He enjoyed holding her close. They fit together like two pieces of a puzzle. He turned his head toward the curve of her neck. It was so very tempting to press a kiss upon that soft skin, but mustering up all his self-restraint, he resisted the urge. He didn't want to ruin their closeness.

Instead, he breathed in her sweet floral scent. He inhaled again, deeper this time, impressing the memory of the addictive scent upon his mind. It would have to be enough for now.

And then she pulled away much too soon. In fact, if it were up to him, he'd never let her go. Wait. Had he really just thought that?

He quickly dismissed the idea. He was getting way ahead of himself. He didn't do long-term relationships. He didn't do commitments. And he certainly didn't do love. He just had to keep reminding himself of that.

He blamed all this emotional stuff on his book. He'd been thinking too long about how to make his hero fall in love. That was it. His brain was still in writing mode. Nothing to worry about. All he needed was a bit of time alone to get his head screwed on straight.

Gianna's eyes sparkled with excitement. She looked so beautiful. There was this funny feeling in his chest, a sensation he'd never experienced before. It warmed him from the inside out.

"We have to go celebrate," she insisted.

He didn't want her to feel obligated to go out of her way for him. He shook his head. "You've already done enough."

"Nonsense. This is huge!" Her voice was filled with genuine excitement. "I know, we'll drive into the city. We'll make it a huge affair."

He couldn't help but smile at the way she was making such a big deal out of his accomplishment. And though he'd originally wanted to jump in the car and go paint up the town, the thought no longer appealed to him. It was enough to celebrate this moment with Gianna. Her excitement was all he needed.

"Thank you," he said. "I really appreciate the thought, but it's getting late and that's a long drive. We'd never be able to get there and back today. And there's Tito to consider."

The smile fell from her face as she considered his words. "I know what we'll do." Her eyes lit up. "It's not as fancy as the city but it's something." Her hands started to move as she talked,

emphasizing her words. "After all, we ha   y something. This is huge. You worked so l   v

"Slow down." He reached out, taking   b pressive hands into his own. "What is it yo in mind?"

"Dinner in the village."

He was surprised by her suggestions. "Ar sure? I know you've been avoiding it as mu possible lately."

Her gaze lowered. "You noticed that, huh

"I did. I've felt really bad about it. I'm so our arrangement put you in such an awkwa position with your family."

Her gaze rose to meet his. "It's not your fault I agreed to this."

"But you regret it?"

She shrugged. She wouldn't say it but he kne she regretted the charade. To his surprise, I didn't. He'd really enjoyed their fake relationsh

"You don't have to worry," he said. "It's ove

Her confused gaze rose to meet his. "Wha

"Our engagement ended when I hit Send."

Her expressive eyes widened. "But what ab your grandparents' anniversary party? The expecting both of us."

"I'll just tell them we broke up."

Her lips pursed together as though consi ing his suggestion. "I don't know."

"I thought you'd be anxious to end this rade. Are you saying you changed your mind

have no choice but to stay together until after the party."

"Are you all right with that?"

Her hesitant gaze met his. "Are you?"

He smiled broadly. "I think a few more days as your adoring fiancé won't be a hardship."

"Adoring, huh?"

Heat flashed over his face. "Must just be the writer in me coming out."

"Uh-huh." She started to walk away.

"Where are you going?"

"To get ready for dinner. I have to look good for my adoring fiancé." And with that, she disappeared down the hallway.

He had a feeling she wasn't going to let him forget his choice of words. Not that he regretted them. Gianna was very special. And he did adore her, but that was a long way from love. Wasn't it? After all, look what had happened to his parents.

Candlelight.

Champagne.

And romantic music.

It had been quite a dinner. Gianna smiled as they strolled back to the villa beneath the bright moonlight. All evening, Dario had played the perfect gentleman. He'd been attentive, entertaining and plied her with compliments. She had to keep reminding herself that it wasn't a real date. Or was it?

This evening was like a dream—one of the dreams she had at night when Dario played a role of being much more than a roommate. She thought of pinching herself to make sure she hadn't nodded off and dreamed up this romantic evening. But her hand was neatly tucked in the crook of his arm and she had no desire to break their physical connection.

"Did you have a good evening?" Dario's deep voice broke into her wayward thoughts.

"It was wonderful. Thank you. But it was your big evening. Did you enjoy it?"

"I've never had such an amazing evening. The food was out of this world. The atmosphere was relaxing. And I was with the most gorgeous woman."

So this was a date. A real date. Her smile broadened. She thought of mentioning it, but she couldn't bring herself to vocalize her thoughts. What if Dario didn't feel the same way? What if it ruined this incredible evening? It was best to keep the thought to herself.

She wanted to squeeze as many happy moments into the short time they had left. The thought dampened her mood, but she quickly brushed it aside. They had tonight and she wasn't ready for it to end. There had to be a way to extend it.

When they reached the house, the ground lights lit up the patio area. The pool lights beckoned to her. She led them to the edge of the pool.

It was a warm evening with barely a breeze. Her heated body would welcome the cool water over her skin, and if Dario was to join her, all the better.

"Why don't we take a dip?" She hoped he'd be agreeable.

"First, I have something to ask you." He turned to her. "I've been meaning to do this all evening but I never found the right moment."

Her heart fluttered in her chest. What was he up to?

And then he knelt down on one knee.

"Dario, what are you doing?" Her heart leaped into her throat.

He pulled a blue velvet box from his pocket and held it out to her. "I'm asking you to be my fake fiancée."

The *fake* part put a damper on her excitement. He was playing a part, but oh, my, what a part. Just the thought that it could have been real was enough to send her heart racing.

"Go ahead. Take it." He moved the box closer to her.

She pressed a hand to her chest. Her fingertips could feel the pounding of her heart. "But… but I can't."

He sent her a reassuring smile. "Yes, you can. It's a gift."

"A gift?" She was confused. "You mean it's not—you know—"

"A diamond ring?"

She nodded, not trusting her voice.

"Why don't you look inside and see?"

Well, it wouldn't hurt just to look. She cautiously reached for the box. All the while, her heart raced. Why was she getting so worked up? The proposal wasn't real.

He chuckled. "Go ahead. It won't bite."

She took the box and, in that moment, she was jealous of the woman that would one day receive a real engagement ring from Dario. Because as much as Dario tried to convince himself that true love didn't exist, she knew one day when he least expected it, he'd fall head over heels in love. And the woman he loved would be the luckiest woman in the world.

Suddenly, her stomach soured. The thought of him sharing a similar moment with another woman made her sad.

"Hey." Dario's voice drew her from her thoughts. He was now standing next to her. When she gazed into his eyes, she saw concern. "It's okay. If you don't like it, we can exchange it."

It took her a moment to realize what he was talking about. She glanced back at the unopened box. She pried the lid back to reveal a large pink stone surrounded by small diamond solitaires.

"It's gorgeous," she said, unable to take her eyes off the stunning piece of jewelry. "Is that a sapphire?"

"It's actually a pink diamond."

Her mouth gaped. It took a moment for her to realize the magnitude of this gift. She turned an accusing gaze his way. "You told me it wasn't a diamond ring."

"Well, um, it's not a traditional diamond ring."

"There's a difference?"

He sent her a sheepish smile. "If I'd have said it was a diamond ring, would you have opened it?"

"No. Absolutely not." A diamond ring shouldn't be a prop for a fake relationship. A diamond ring meant eternal love that could make it through the fires that life threw at a couple. It wasn't a trivial piece of jewelry.

His brows rose. "You seem mighty certain of that. I mean, don't all women love diamonds?"

"I don't know about all women, but this one thinks a diamond ring should come with love and the promise of forever."

The color drained from his face. "I see. Well, will a heartfelt thank-you be enough?"

She closed the box and handed it back to him. "Dario, take it back. It's way too much."

His hand closed over hers. His touch was gentle and warm. She loved the way his skin felt against hers. She lifted her gaze to meet his. She meant to say something but as their gazes held, the words vanished from her mind.

His gaze dipped to her lips. Her heart raced

as he drew her hand closer until it was pressed to his solid chest. She naturally stepped closer.

When he spoke, his voice was low and full of desire. "You do know I want to kiss you, don't you?"

She gave a slight nod as his gaze continued to hold hers.

With his free hand, he reached out to her. The backs of his fingers brushed lightly over her cheek. "And you realize this is a mistake?"

She once more attempted to speak but the words got clogged in her throat. Instead, she nodded once more.

He lowered his head just as she lifted up on her tiptoes. Their lips pressed to each other. She had waited so long for this moment—the feel of his touch. It was so much better than the memory that kept her awake at night.

His arms wrapped around her like steel bands, anchoring her to him. She released the ring box into his hand and then pressed both hands to his chest. Her fingers worked their way slowly up toward his broad shoulders, taking in all the contours of his muscles. He was the full package—brains and brawn.

But then he pulled back. Uncertainty showed in his eyes. She liked that he didn't automatically assume they'd be spending the night together, though she knew that's where this evening was headed. She just didn't want to rush things. This was too good not to be savored.

Because when Dario went back to his life and she was once more sleeping in a tent while working with a new film crew, she wanted to have the memories to look back on. She knew there would never be another man in her life like Dario.

He stepped back. He raked his fingers through his hair. "We should probably stop there."

"Really? Are you sure?" At that moment, she was feeling daring. She slipped a strap of her summer dress down over her shoulder.

Desire flared in his dark eyes. "Gianna, what are you doing?"

"What do you think I'm doing?"

"I... I don't know."

His avid interest drove her onward. She slipped the other strap down over her shoulder. "It's awfully hot out here." It was no lie. When he looked at her like that, it set her body afire. "Don't you think?"

He nodded but no words were spoken.

She smiled. She reached behind her and released the zipper. Her dress swished to the ground. The breath caught in her lungs. Had she gone too far?

She stood there in her black halter bra, her matching lacy boy shorts and a pair of high heels. She'd never done anything like this before. Her heart pounded as her palms grew moist. She had absolutely no idea what Dario's reaction would be. She knew how she wanted him to react, but right now his wide-eyed stare said she'd surprised both of them.

And then he smiled. A big ole smile lit up his whole face.

She smiled too, enjoying having his full attention. She just had to keep up this act a little longer and then she'd make a grand exit. Because standing here in her underwear, which, granted, provided more covering than her bikini, was still a bit—okay, a lot—nerve-racking.

She resisted the urge to rush as she kicked off her heels. She'd never played a seductress before and she was finding it so much fun. She stepped closer to him, as though she were going to have her way with him, but then she dove into the pool.

When she emerged and swiped the water from her face, she found Dario standing at the pool's edge with a confused look upon his face.

"The water's nice," she said, "why don't you join me?"

She didn't have to ask twice. He stripped down to his boxers and dove in. He swam up to her. "You are a tease."

"Am I?" She grinned at him.

When he reached out to her, she swam away. When he sent her another confused look, she said, "Half of the fun is the chase."

A knowing smile lit up his face. Then he took off after her. He caught her hand here and her leg there. Each time she escaped. She had a feeling he was intentionally letting her get away.

All the while, her pulse raced with excitement. She knew what was at the end of the chase, an amazing night wrapped in his arms.

When she finally emerged at the end of the pool, where they'd first dove in, she let him catch up to her. Playing cat and mouse was fine for a time, but she was in the mood to be caught now.

He snaked an arm around her waist and pulled her close. "You can't get away now."

"I don't want to get away now." Her fingertip followed a drop of water as it slid down his bare chest.

"I wasn't sure before but now I know for certain you're a tease."

She shook her head. "Am not. If I were, I wouldn't have waited here for you to catch up to me." She slid her arms up around his neck and then raised her legs, wrapping them around his waist. "It seems to me you're the one that has been caught."

He moaned. "You can catch me anytime you want."

And then he claimed her lips once more. There was fire in his kiss—a driving desire that she met with a need of her own. She may not be his real fiancée, but just for tonight, they'd pretend.

CHAPTER FOURTEEN

THE BIG DAY had arrived.

They were getting an early start as there was so much to do. Gianna was so nervous that she could barely eat more than some bread. Her stomach was tied up in knots. She wasn't sure which made her more nervous: the awards at the photography competition and living up to her grandmother's legacy or meeting Dario's entire family for the first time. Both were quite daunting events.

But she knew those weren't the only reasons she was so worked up that morning. There was also the tiny thing about her sleeping with Dario. Just the mere thought of their intimate time together sent her heart racing and made her face burning hot.

Even though their time together was coming to a close after the weekend with both of their families, they'd agreed to have an amicable, very mature breakup.

Although it didn't feel like things were ending. It felt like something new was just beginning. Was that possible? Did Dario feel the same way? Or was she just blowing last night's seduction out of proportion?

Dario appeared before her in dark jeans, a light blue button-up and a blue blazer with dark sunglasses resting on top of his head. He looked like he'd just stepped off a fashion runway. And then her gaze settled on his lips. Oh, those lips…

"You look beautiful." His voice interrupted the beginning of her fantasy.

"Thank you." Heat swirled in her chest and rushed up to engulf her cheeks. She glanced down, hoping he wouldn't see her blush. But then she decided to get the hard part over with. She lifted her chin slightly, enough to meet his gaze. "About last night—"

"We can talk about it later. Right now, we have a competition to get you too." He didn't act any different after their night together. "Are you ready to go?"

"I just have to grab my purse. What about my things for the weekend?" She had a bag with her makeup and other essentials. There was also a garment bag with her dress. Another bag contained her shoes. And then one special surprise for Dario, but he wouldn't get it until later. "Are we going straight from the Botanical Gardens to Verona?"

He glanced at all her things and smiled. "Leave

them. We can't take Tito to the Botanical Gardens so we'll get them when we pick him up."

"Okay. I'm ready. I guess."

"You guess." He approached her and gazed into her eyes. "What are you worried about?"

"That I'm making a fool of myself. I don't know why I ever thought I was as good a photographer as my grandmother. She had a special talent when it came to capturing specific moments on film. She won this competition many times."

"And you have the same talent."

"How would you know? I didn't even let you see my entry. What if it's pedestrian?"

"Pedestrian? Really? We're going with the big words now?"

She shook her head. "You know what I mean. What if the photo is uninspiring?"

"I know what the word means. I just can't believe you're doubting yourself."

"Well, you've been doubting yourself about the book and I know for a fact you're a talented author."

He smiled. "Touché. Now let's go or I'm leaving you here. I'm dying to see your entry since you wouldn't give me a sneak peek. I know it's going to be amazing."

She smiled at his enthusiasm. He made her feel so much better. If she failed at the competition, at least she wouldn't be there alone. There was something very comforting about having Dario by her side. It was as if they'd always been together.

He truly was excited for her.

The ferry ride to Fiorire Island in the southern portion of Lake Como seemed to take forever, even though it was quite a short ride. But Dario was anxious to see Gianna's entry. He'd seen some of her other work—the pieces she said weren't her best. If that hadn't been her best, he couldn't imagine how amazing her entry must be.

He reached out and took her hand as they made their way up the walk to the stately villa nestled in the middle of the colorful and fragrant botanical garden. Once at the door, he had to release her hand in order to purchase their tickets. And then they were given a guide that Gianna immediately started to scan. His chance of holding her hand once more had slipped away.

He focused on reading the brochure. It spoke of the history of the small island. The massive building they were standing in had once been a villa for royalty. Late in the twentieth century the small private island had been donated to a historical preservation group.

For exactly two weeks each year, the museum removed their normal exhibits in order to display the prestigious entries for the international photography competition. Today, the place was packed with visitors.

"Let's just cut to your section," Dario suggested.

She shook her head. "We should just stay in line. We'll get there."

He shifted his weight from one foot to the other. The advantage of being tall was being able to see over a crowd. There were a lot people ahead of them, all following between the two red velvet ropes. This was going to take forever.

"Don't you want to know how you did?" he asked.

"Of course, I do. But I'd also like to see some of the other entries."

"We could come back another time to see them."

She frowned at him. He quieted down. He hadn't realized just how truly excited he was for her until they'd arrived. All this time she'd been cheering him on with his book and now it was his turn to cheer her on.

He worried that if for some unexpected reason she didn't do well with the competition, she wouldn't pursue her gift as a photographer. And that worried him. He'd seen over the past weeks how it excited her. Something that made you want to get out of bed before the sun was a true passion, in his way of thinking. It's the way he felt about his writing. He didn't want to see her lose that passion.

The line slowly crept forward. Gianna pointed

out different aspects of the photos and tried to explain to him about the various lens and filters that were used, but most of it went over his head.

They continued moving. He wasn't even sure what category she'd entered. Gianna had kept everything very hush-hush. She said she didn't want to do anything to jinx herself. He didn't believe in that stuff, but he hadn't argued. And then they approached the section for plants.

"This is it," Gianna whispered as she clasped her hands together.

"You've got this."

They stepped into the room where people were pointing and whispering, as people do in a museum. His gaze moved around the wall, trying to figure out which photo was Gianna's. He had to admit that all the entries were impressive, some more so than others.

"There it is." She pointed halfway around the room.

This time he didn't ask her permission, he simply grabbed her hand, lifted the velvet rope and cut through the center of the room.

"What are you doing?" Gianna looked panicked.

"Sir, you have to follow the line," a security guard said.

"But you don't understand, that's my girlfriend's print on the wall." It wasn't until the words were spoken that he realized he'd publicly called Gianna his girlfriend. And he had no desire to take it back. "And we've been waiting forever to see it."

The guard was a nice young man. "Okay. But just this once. Which one is it?"

Gianna pointed to what looked something like a reddish-orange daisy with a violet center. They couldn't see the whole thing as there were people in front of it, pointing and nodding. But from the distance, Dario couldn't see an award. His heart sunk. Was it possible she hadn't placed in the competition?

He started to think of all the things he could say to boost her up should the worst happen. After all, this was her first competition. And these were just one set of judges. What did they know?

Gianna tightened her grip on his hand. He glanced at her to see what she wanted, but her attention was solely focused on the wall hanging.

And then the people moved on, giving them full view of the print. They stepped closer. The next people in line were excited to know that Gianna was the photographer. They welcomed them to get in line in front of them.

Beside the print was a little shelf with a crystal frame and inside was a small plaque with the competition's name, the year, Gianna's name and the word *WINNER*.

"You did it!" Dario didn't care if he'd announced it too loud.

She turned to him with tears of joy in her eyes. "My grandmother would be so happy."

He leaned over and kissed her. He hadn't put any thought into it. It happened naturally as though they'd been doing it for years. And when she kissed him back, his heart swelled.

When he pulled back, he said, "I'm so proud of you."

"Thank you." She sniffled and swiped away the tears that had spilled onto her cheeks.

"You don't have to leave home for work if you don't want to. This can be the beginning of your photography business."

Excitement glittered in her eyes. "You think so?"

"I always believed you can do whatever you set your mind to."

This time, she lifted up on her tiptoes and gave him a quick kiss.

When she pulled away, he took a closer look at the winning entry. The red and oranges of the daisy-like petals were vibrant and the morning dew sparkled. The flower was the central focus of the piece, but in the background, rays of sunshine showered down upon the flower, making it practically glow. And there was a drop of dew falling from the flower. It was small but when he focused in on it, he noticed that within the droplet was a tiny mirror image of the flower. He was certain there were other amazing details that his untrained eyes were missing, but to him the piece was perfection.

When he turned to say something to Gianna, he found her surrounded by people congratulating her and asking for her business card. She said she didn't have any with her. It looked like she needed to print some because she was going into business. His smile broadened.

Her fans wanted to purchase her work. And he couldn't have been happier for her. Gianna had found her passion and he knew she would be successful at it. Best of all, she was glowing with happiness.

Part one of the day had been an utter success.

Part two was quite likely to be the opposite.

Gianna's stomach shivered with nerves as Dario, Tito and herself stepped into his grandparents' home, which was even larger and grander than the museum on Fiorire Island. She glanced down, noticing the slight tremor in her hands. What in the world was she getting so worked up for? It wasn't even like they were a real couple. Okay, so maybe things had gotten a little out of control—or rather a whole lot out of delicious control last night. She smiled as she recalled waking up in Dario's arms.

She leaned closer to Dario and whispered, "They're going to hate me."

He glanced over at her. In his eyes, she saw calm reassurance. "It doesn't matter what they think because to me, you're the best. And if they can't see that, it's their loss."

His kind words filled her heart until it was overflowing. How exactly had this very thoughtful and sweet man avoided a commitment all this time? Because from what she could see, aside from his endless hours hiding away writing, he was amazing. Any woman would be lucky to have him in her life.

Her gaze dipped. The burn of jealousy started in the pit of her stomach as she imagined the willowy figure of the smiling woman who would one day stand here with him and meet his grandparents as his real and dearly loved fiancée.

Dario placed a finger beneath her chin and lifted until their gazes met. "Stop worrying. I'll be right here beside you the whole time."

Their gazes held longer than necessary. She found a sense of peace in his presence and his reassuring words. But as she stared deeper into his eyes, she saw something else. Desire.

Her heart thump-thumped. In that moment, she forgot they were standing in the grand foyer of his grandparents' villa. For the moment, there was just him and her. The pounding of her heart drowned out her worries. The tip of her tongue swiped over her dry lips. His eyes dilated as he watched her. And she reveled in the fact that she could turn him on so quickly.

His head lowered as hers lifted. Their lips met in the middle. He pulled her snugly into his arms. She reached up, wrapping her arms around his neck and lacing her fingers together before drawing him closer.

Why did this feel so right? It shouldn't be that way. After all, they weren't a real couple. But then again, none of her relationships had been like this one. Maybe that had been her problem—

Someone cleared their throat.

They sprang apart. Heat engulfed her whole face. When she glanced over to see an older couple approaching them, she wanted to melt into the marble floor. What had she been thinking? Oh, yes, how much she wanted to kiss Dario over and over again. Talk about bad timing.

Dario reached for her hand, taking it in his. With his other hand, he tugged on Tito's leash, drawing him close. Dario then gave Gianna a firm but reassuring squeeze. She naturally leaned into his side, enjoying the feel of his muscled arm pressed up against her. It felt natural, as though they'd done it many times.

It wasn't until his grandmother's eyes momentarily widened that she realized exactly what she'd done. She straightened, but Dario didn't release his hold on her hand. He kept his fingers wrapped securely around hers. Originally, she'd thought he'd done it to comfort her, but now she wondered if he too needed some support while facing his grandparents.

"Dario, it's about time you came home." His grandmother's face was devoid of emotion until she caught sight of Tito. A distinct frown marred her face. She pointed at Tito. "What's he doing here?"

"I don't have anyone to watch him for the weekend. Tito stays or we go."

His grandmother's pointed stare met his. After a moment, she said, "He can stay so long as he behaves."

"He will." Dario looked down at Tito who was sitting next to him. "You're a good boy, right?"

Woof.

Everyone smiled except his grandparents. Gianna couldn't help but think how strange this cool and aloof greeting was between Dario and his grandparents. Her family was quite the opposite. They were loud and boisterous. Hugs and kisses were exchanged both coming and going.

His grandfather frowned. "You haven't been at the office."

"It's good to see you both." Dario did his best to sound upbeat. "I've missed you."

At last, his grandmother cracked a slight smile. "It's so good to have you home. You've been gone too long." His grandmother's gaze moved to Gianna.

Dario cleared his throat. "Nonna and Nonno, I'd like to introduce you to Gianna Cappellini." He gripped her hand tighter, as though he were nervous. "She's an award-winning photographer. And she's my fiancée." He paused to flash her a big smile. "Gianna, these are my grandparents, Giuseppe and Rosmunda Marchello."

When the older woman held out a hand to her, Gianna thought she meant to shake hands, but the woman grasped her hand and pulled her forward. Gianna reluctantly let go of her grip on Dario's hand and now she felt adrift. What was his grandmother up to?

"Let me have a look at you," his grandmother said. She looked her up and down.

Then her gaze moved between Gianna and Dario. "I think you two will make adorable children together."

"Nonna!" Dario's face filled with color.

Gianna couldn't help but smile. She hadn't considered kids before but with his height and good looks, she believed his grandmother was onto something. Not that they were going to have children now or ever. But the horrified look on his face had Gianna smothering a laugh.

His grandmother scoffed at his reaction. "Honestly, you'd think I'd said something that surprised you. It's only natural you two will have a child."

"Nonna, I don't think now is the time to discuss this." Dario's tone was soft but firm.

"What is your name?" his grandfather asked.

She swallowed. "Gianna."

He shook his head. "I mean your family's name."

"Cappellini."

His gray brows drew together and then he turned to his wife. "Do we know any Cappellinis?"

The woman paused as though to give the question due consideration. "I don't believe we do."

His grandfather turned back to her. "What areas are your parents involved?"

Maybe it was the loud pounding of her heart or her racing pulse but she didn't understand the question. She glanced at Dario for clarification.

Thankfully, he was paying attention. "He wants to know what your parents do for a living."

Well, why didn't he just say that to begin with? She smiled at the older gentleman. "My father owns a market and my mother runs the office for him."

"A market?" his grandfather said, as though he hadn't heard her correctly.

She forced a smile to her lips and nodded. Her family may not be nearly as impressive as the Marchellos but Gianna was proud of her parents. She went on to explain that it was the largest market in their village and how it had been there for close to thirty years. Her father had no intention of retiring. He loved the daily interaction with the community.

His grandfather didn't utter a single acknowledgment to her but rather turned to Dario. "We need to speak."

Gianna felt the sting of an unspoken insult. She didn't live up to his grandfather's expectations. She tried to tell herself it didn't matter as they weren't truly engaged anyway, but it didn't ease the pain that dug at her. The sooner this weekend was over, the better.

"It'll have to wait," Dario's grandmother said. "We need to discuss the wedding plans."

At least his grandmother wasn't opposed to their relationship. It helped ease Gianna's discomfort.

"Nonna," Dario said, "this weekend isn't supposed to be about our engagement. It's about you and Nonno."

"Nonsense. There's enough time for both." His grandmother's eyes lit up and the slight smile lifted into a full one that lit up her whole face. "Now, if we could just find your brother a wife."

"Don't waste your time," Dario said. "He's married to his work."

"Thankfully, someone is," his grandfather

grumped. "If it were up to you, there wouldn't be any business."

She glanced at Dario to find his shoulders rigid and his face drawn. His lips were pressed in a firm line as a muscle in his cheek twitched. She sensed he was fighting to hold back a heated response. Suddenly, Gianna didn't feel so bad that his grandfather found her and her family so unworthy of a Marchello. No one lived up to the older man's expectations.

Still, she couldn't just stand by and let his grandfather put down Dario. "Your grandson has worked very hard over the past month."

"Humph!" The man crossed his arms as his gaze narrowed on her. "Like you would know anything about it."

Dario glanced at her and gave a firm shake of his head. He must have thought she was about to spill his secret about his writing. She would never do that to him.

She turned back to his grandfather, who was scowling. It appeared he wasn't used to people standing up to him. Well, he better get used to it because she didn't back down when someone she cared about was being attacked.

"I know your grandson worked remotely. He had his business phone forwarded to his cell phone and he was on his laptop at all hours dealing with whatever came up at the office while his brother was away."

His grandfather's brows rose and then he turned to his grandson. "Is this true?"

Dario nodded. "Everything is under control."

"And you'll be back in the office on Monday?"

Gianna knew that was the very last place Dario wanted to be. She didn't understand why he didn't just tell them that he was a best-selling author. Why would he hide something like that? She was so proud of him that she was about to burst.

"Yes, Nonno. I'll be there."

"Good." His grandfather turned and walked away.

"Now we can get started," Nonna said.

"Can we do it later?" Dario asked. "I promised Gianna I'd show her around."

His grandmother hesitated and then nodded. "Go. Have a good time. Dinner will be promptly at seven and we will be having guests."

Dario showed her to the upstairs. They stopped outside a guest room. Just then the door swung open. A maid stepped into the hallway. Her eyes widened upon spotting them.

Gianna's gaze lowered to her luggage, which was in the maid's hands. "Where are you taking my things?"

"I was told to move them to Mr. Marchello's suite. Is that not right?"

Gianna looked at him for help. She had no idea what to say. Now that their engagement was known, it was expected that they'd share a room—a bed. Heat crept into her cheeks.

As the maid waited for instructions, Dario said, "Yes, that's right. Thank you."

The young woman smiled and nodded before she rushed off. They followed her to a room at the end of the hallway. They told the maid they'd take care of hanging their own things.

Gianna couldn't believe she was in Dario's inner sanctum—the place where he'd grown up. She didn't know what she'd been expecting. It certainly wasn't the sparsely decorated light taupe walls with landscape portraits. This was a boy's room?

Her gaze moved to the two dressers. There was a framed photo of a football team. She drew near and picked it up. "Which one is you?"

He pointed to the boy in the center with the ball in his hands. She noticed he was smiling for the camera.

"You were a cute kid." She returned the photo to where she'd found it.

She turned and found large wooden bookcases, each shelf crammed with books—some standing and some lying on their sides. There was no room left on any of the shelves.

"You weren't kidding about your love of reading."

"That's not all of them. Just my favorites." He cleared his throat. "I'm sorry about all of this."

She turned her attention back to him. "Is your family always that way?"

He shrugged. "Pretty much."

"Why didn't you just tell them about your writing?"

"I will. When the time is right."

She had a feeling that was just an excuse. "When will that be?"

He lowered his voice to a very soft whisper. "As soon as book two is sold."

"Won't that be a while?"

"I don't know." His face was marred with worry lines. "They were really anxious for it so they might read it right away. But I don't know if they'll like it. It's so different from the first book."

"Relax." She sent him a reassuring smile. "It's a good thing that it's different. Trust me."

"You didn't read it after the revisions."

"But I know you have crazy skills with words. I have faith that you wrote a fantastic book." She moved forward and gave him a hug. "I'm so proud of you."

His arms wrapped around her, pulling her a little closer. The action felt so natural, as though they did it all the time. And she was very tempted to lift her face and claim his lips, so they could pick up where they'd left off before.

But that wasn't what they were here to do. Their one-night fling was over. They were here to put on a show just until his grandparents' big celebration weekend was over. Then they too would be over. The thought left a heaviness in her chest.

Before things got out of control again, she withdrew from his arms. "I should get freshened up." She hesitated. "I guess I should have asked before—how many times will we be expected to dress for an event?"

"Tonight. Tomorrow afternoon and then again in the evening. The same for Saturday. And then Sunday just for the afternoon."

"Oh." She mentally calculated what she had in her wardrobe. "I didn't bring enough dresses to wear."

"Don't worry. We can get whatever you need in the city. I'm going to take Tito for a quick walk. Do you need anything before I go?"

She shook her head.

"I'll be back shortly." With Tito next to him, Dario headed for the door.

Gianna took the time alone to figure out where to put the surprise she'd brought for him. She looked in the closet, but found it too empty. He'd spot it immediately. There also wasn't enough room behind either dresser. She settled for placing it under the bed. What were the chances he'd look under there?

CHAPTER FIFTEEN

ALONE AT LAST.

Dario was quickly realizing how soon his time with Gianna would end. The whole month had gone by much too fast. But now that the book was complete, he didn't have a reason to return to Gemma with her. At least not yet...

If he'd had any doubts about how well suited they were for each other, their night together had been the final deciding factor. It was though they'd been made for each other.

With one of the household staff looking after Tito, Dario was free to show Gianna around his old haunts. As they strolled through Verona, he glanced down at their clasped hands. She was still wearing his ring. He smiled. He still had time to turn this all around—a chance to show her that not all men were like her ex. After all, she'd taught Dario that true love exists in books; maybe it existed in real life too.

"You know you really don't have to do this." Gianna's voice drew him from his thoughts.

"Do what?"

"Spend your afternoon showing me around. I'm sure you have plenty of other things you'd rather be doing."

"You mean like being closed up in the study with my grandfather going over inventory reports or ad campaigns and sales figures." He shook his head. "I'd much rather be out here in the sunshine, showing you my city."

She glanced at him. Their gazes connected and held for a second too long before she turned her head. "And a beautiful city it is."

"But you haven't seen much of it yet." He kept walking to a bustling market spot. "This is Piazza delle Erbe, otherwise known as the Square of Herbs."

She glanced around the picturesque town square surrounded by historic buildings—oh, the stories they could tell if they could speak. The piazza was overlooked by a tall clock tower. And in the center of the square was a beautiful fountain. And surrounding it were shops and cozy cafés. Gianna was anxious to visit each storefront, tented vendor and restaurant. She wanted to take it all in.

But Dario was headed for the center of the square where tented booths were being visited by a large number of leisurely customers. Young and old alike visited the square. It was vibrant and yet somehow homey. Like her village in the south of Italy. It wasn't until she left it that she realized how much she loved it.

Gianna listened to the hubbub of conversation as she inhaled the delicious aromas drifting into the square from the surrounding restaurants. She couldn't stop smiling as they continued to walk.

Some people had cloth bags hung from their arms stuffed full of their wonderful finds. Others had woven baskets full of fruits and vegetables. There was hardly a soul that hadn't found something to buy.

Dario stopped and bought them each a refreshment. Her dry throat welcomed the sweet drink. They moved about the square, slowly walking from stand to stand, inspecting all the abundant produce. Other people were standing off to the side, talking amongst themselves, smiling and laughing. It was definitely a welcoming place. A place to meet up with old friends and to make new ones.

"I like it here," she said, "It's like bringing a bit of the village life into the big city."

He nodded in agreement. "This is a very special spot for my family."

"Because you sell spices?"

He nodded. "This square is where my great-grandfather started Marchello Spices. He'd bring his herbs to market and people would rave about them. Every week he'd sell out. And as his business grew, he incorporated in more spices and herbs."

She walked with Dario among the vendors, admiring their fresh fruit and vegetables. And then she came to a stop in front of the Marchello Spices stand. She turned to him. "You still keep a stand here, even though your company is so big?"

He smiled and nodded. "My grandfather thought it was foolish and a waste of time and money, but my brother and I disagreed. We thought we should hold on to our heritage and always remember where we started."

She smiled at him. "I think it's wonderful that you retain a bit of your past. Heritage is important."

"Is that why you moved into your grandmother's home and followed in her footsteps with photography?"

She'd never really thought of it that way. "I don't know if I was trying to take after her as much as photography is just a part of me. I feel most comfortable behind the lens of a camera. Framing out snippets of life that tell a story excites me. And as for her house, well, I've loved it there since I was a kid and we'd go to visit. It's just so peaceful."

He smiled at her. "I have to agree with you. I might need to come back and visit when I write my next book."

Hope swelled in her chest. She told herself it

was the hope that he'd continue writing and not the hope that he'd come spend more time with her. "You said when not if. Does that mean you'll keep writing?"

He nodded. "Even if my current submission doesn't sell—"

"It will."

His brows lifted in surprise at her outburst but then he smiled. "Even so, I just can't imagine my life without writing. It's now a part of me. It's something I look forward to each day. And when I'm not writing, I'm thinking about writing or plotting out the next scene in my head."

"That sounds so exciting."

"Exciting and exhausting because sometimes there's no turning off my imagination until I sit down and write out some notes so I don't forget what I came up with."

Gianna stepped up to the Marchello stand where there were so many spices and herbs to choose from. The truth was that she'd grown up with Marchello spices in her parents' kitchen. The red, green and white labels were a staple, but what she didn't realize was how extensive Marchello's inventory was until now.

"What are you doing?" Dario asked.

"What does it look like? I'm shopping."

"But you don't have to buy those things just because they're ours."

"I'm not. But there are some things here that I've never seen in the store."

He nodded in understanding. "That's because the stores will only take the main staples of our collection—the big sellers. We used to be able to let the consumers try the products before buying them."

"How was that?"

"They used to be in restaurants where guests could choose from a caddy of different spices to add to their pasta. And they even sold containers of them."

"Wait. I remember now. They were in Carla's family's restaurants."

He nodded. "Until eleven years ago."

"What happened then?"

"I don't know all the details, but Carlo Falco and my grandfather used to be friends. They'd play cards together. Something happened and they've never spoken since."

"I'm sorry that happened."

"So am I. When Franco and I took over the company five years ago, we tried getting our products back in Falco's Fresco Ristorante but Carla's father wouldn't hear of it. When our grandfather found out what we were up to, he got so irate that I thought he was going to have a heart attack. That's when I started taking my writing seriously. Tensions were so high in the family that I needed a way to escape, if you will."

"I feel the same way about my photography. There's just something about being one-on-one with nature."

"What about human subjects?"

She shrugged. "It's okay if I just randomly snap a photo here or there."

"Like you did when I was writing?"

"Exactly. The candid, unposed images are what I like. But I'm not one to open a studio and deal with people regularly." She shook her head. "That's definitely not for me. What about you and your company? What will you do with the spices that don't make it into the stores?"

"Well, we do sell the full line of spices and herbs online, but the sales aren't sustainable. And if the company doesn't find a more reliable, hands-on approach to selling those specialty items, I'm afraid we'll have to cease their production."

Gianna reached in her bag and pulled out the bottle of specially mixed herbs she'd just purchased. "This was my favorite when I was a kid."

"It's one that will be cut from production. I'm sorry."

She frowned as she put it back in her purse. "Maybe I should go back and get more."

When she turned around, he reached out, placing a hand on her arm. He smiled and shook his head. "Relax. You can still get it online. And we're not making those dreadful decisions just yet. My brother is spending a great deal of time traveling and meeting with other restaurant owners to get the more select items in front of customers."

"I hope he's successful."

"I do too. But Falco's Fresco Ristorante is the biggest and most successful chain in the country. If only we could figure out what caused the rift between the two men, maybe we could patch things up and get back to business."

"I'd help you if I could, but this is the first I'm hearing of it." Gianna's phone buzzed. "Sorry. It's Carla."

"Not a problem." He continued browsing the stands while she moved off to the side to take the call.

"Hi. What's going on?"

"I just got to the city. Are you at Dario's grandparents' estate?"

"Actually, I'm in the city. I need to find a couple of dresses—"

"Say no more. We can meet for a late lunch and then I can take you to my favorite shops."

Carla gave her the address of the café and then rushed off the phone.

Gianna returned to Dario, who just finished a brief conversation with an older gentleman. "Sorry about that."

"No problem. It gave me a chance to say hello to some old friends. Is everything okay?"

"Yes. Carla wants to meet up for lunch and then go shopping. I hope you don't mind."

"Not at all. My grandfather wants to have a talk. He appeared to have something serious on his mind. I should go back and do that now before the festivities begin."

"Oh, you don't want to join us for lunch?" She wasn't ready to see him go, not yet.

"I'll just eat back at the villa. I can drop you off on my way."

She shook her head. "I looked it up on my phone. It's not far from here and it's such a beautiful day, I'd like to walk. I hope things go well with your grandfather."

He nodded in agreement. "If you need me, I'm just a phone call away."

They parted there in the piazza. She was disappointed they hadn't gotten to explore more of Verona together. She immediately told herself that they'd do it another time. And in the next breath, she remembered there wouldn't be another time. Their time together was almost over and the thought weighed heavy on her heart.

CHAPTER SIXTEEN

She missed Dario already.

It was silly. But it was true.

The walk to the café had been just what she'd needed before meeting up with her cousin. Because today she was going to confess her secret. She just couldn't let Carla find out with everyone else that her engagement had all been a sham.

But first, Gianna decided to focus on something positive. "I have some news."

"You set a wedding date?"

She smiled and shook her head. "I won the photography contest at the Fiorire Botanical Gardens."

"Congratulations! I'm so happy for you." Carla studied her. "Why aren't you more excited about the win?"

"I'm happy." Gianna reached for a tall glass of tea. "I'm just tired, I guess."

"Oh, my!" Carla's face lit up. "You got the ring. Let me see."

Gianna had momentarily forgotten that she

was wearing it. Dario had placed it on her finger at some point during their night together. And now she didn't have the heart to take it off. The ring was just so beautiful. And Dario had insisted there was a no-return policy, so he was stuck with it unless she accepted it as a token of his greatest appreciation for all she'd done to help make his dreams come true.

As she held the ring out for Carla, Gianna admired it too. It may not have come with a promise of eternal love but it had come with what she hoped was an abiding friendship and maybe a little more.

"Wow! That's some ring." Carla sent her a knowing smile over the small café table. "Why didn't you bring him to lunch? I'd have loved to see him again."

"I didn't want to pressure him. He had an important meeting."

"I bet he would have dropped everything for you. I've seen the way he looks at you. He's crazy about you."

It had been on the tip of her tongue to ask him, but she'd stood her ground and resisted her urge. One night together did not make a couple. But then she realized that she hadn't fessed up to her cousin about her fake engagement. And the guilt weighed on her. With the light lunch complete, now was the time to fess up.

"What is it?" Carla prompted.

Gianna's hesitant gaze met her cousin's. "There's something I need to tell you."

And now that she was saying the words, she wondered if she was going to mess up another relationship in her life. After all, there was no guarantee that her cousin was going to forgive her.

Carla's smile faltered. "Oh, no. Did something happen with you and Dario? Please say it isn't so." When Gianna didn't immediately respond, Carla said, "Gianna? You're starting to worry me."

Gianna drew in a deep breath but it did absolutely nothing to calm her racing heart. She never should have gone along with the fake engagement. She could just add it to her growing list of regrets.

"Oh, no." Carla's eyes displayed her concern. "Whatever it is, you two can fix it. He loves you. After all, look at that engagement ring he gave you."

"That's just it. It's not an engagement ring."

"What? I don't understand." Carla rested her elbows on the table and leaned forward. "Are you trying to say that you two have broken up?"

"It's worse than that."

"What could be worse?"

It took all her resolve to tilt her chin upward ever so slightly, just enough to meet her cousin's worried gaze. "We were never truly engaged."

"What?" Carla leaned back in her chair as

though the air had just gone out of her. "But what about the ring?"

"It…it's a thank-you gift. Nothing more."

"You mean this whole time when you said you were getting married, it was lie."

Gianna wanted to turn away from the hurt emanating from her cousin's eyes, but she wouldn't let herself off that easy. She kept meeting her cousin's gaze. "In the beginning, it wasn't a lie."

"So you were engaged to Dario? For real?"

She shook her head. "It was another guy. We worked together. It was a whirlwind romance. I should have known it all moved too quickly, but he was so sweet, so convinced that everything would work out just the way it was supposed to. And I guess in a way it has."

"This guy, he was someone that traveled with you from the jungles of Africa to the icy cold Antarctica?"

She nodded. "He was the host of the series."

Carla's mouth formed an O.

"He'd just broken up with someone and so had I. At first, we were just there for each other, bolstering each other through the painful aftermath. I think in part it was a case of proximity. We shared the same campsites and all of our meals. Let me tell you, there aren't many people out in the wilderness to speak to."

"I can only imagine. So you were really into him?"

She nodded. "At least I thought I was. We had so much in common. And we seemed to want the same things in the future."

"Seemed to?"

Gianna glanced down at the red-and-white-check tablecloth. "I have this bad habit of letting myself get caught up in someone else's life and aligning my desires with theirs. And once we're apart, I realize how skewed my thinking has become."

"Why did you two break up? Did you figure out he was a jerk?"

Gianna shook her head. "He went back to his ex."

"Definitely a jerk! You must be so mad at him."

"I was in the beginning. I was furious. But then I realized it was for the best. I was so tired of living out of a duffel bag and sleeping on the hard ground. I've been running away from home long enough. I thought there was no reason to be here, if I didn't have anyone to share my life with."

"And now?"

"Now, I know that to be truly happy, I have to make a life for myself."

"So why did you let me go on about you and Dario being engaged. And then I got Franco to believe it. Wait. Does he know you two aren't really together?" Color rushed to Carla's cheeks as her thoughts turned to Franco. "He must think I'm such a dolt. I just went on and on about what a great couple you two make—"

"Relax. He still thinks we're engaged."

Carla sighed. "That's good. Not about him not knowing the truth, but that he doesn't think I'm totally clueless. And there's your parents. I might have let it slip…"

"It's okay. I plan to talk to them when they arrive for the party. I didn't feel right about doing it on the phone."

"I was so certain you two were in love. Are you? In love, that is?"

"No!" The rushed answer only made the awkward moment that much more uncomfortable. This time it was Gianna's turn to have heat rush to her cheeks. "Definitely not."

Carla arched a fine penciled brow. "Are you sure about that?"

"Positive!" Again with the too-quick answer.

"He really is a looker," Carla said.

But two could play at this game. "So is his brother, Franco. I noticed how you were looking at him."

Carla glanced away as she fidgeted with her discarded linen napkin. "There's nothing there. He was far too anxious to fly away on business."

"But he will be at his grandparents' anniversary party—"

"Stop." Carla pursed her lips as though choosing her next words carefully. "We were talking about you, not me."

So Carla had been attracted to Franco. Interesting. Very interesting. Gianna wondered what it'd take to get those two together. But as soon as the thought came to her, she dismissed it. From the little she knew of Franco, he was much too intense for her cousin.

Gianna fidgeted with her discarded napkin. "Anyway, I just wanted to say I am sorry for not correcting you when you assumed Dario was my fiancé."

"Why didn't you correct me?"

Gianna shrugged again. Finding words were hard for her. She didn't want to say the wrong thing and make this harder for her cousin to forgive her. She was her best friend in the whole world. Then her thoughts shifted to Dario. He had suddenly become her closest friend. She'd told things to him that she hadn't even told Carla. What was she going to do without him in her life?

"Gianna?" Carla waved a hand in front of her to gain her attention. "Why did you keep up the charade?"

"Because I didn't want to look like a two-time failure. I am so pathetic when it comes to relationships."

"No, you're not. Those men just didn't know how great you are. If they did, they'd have never let you go." Carla leaned forward with sympathy in her eyes. "Speaking of which, I know this great guy—"

"No. Stop." Gianna waved off her cousin. "I don't need a pity date."

"But you don't understand. He's a really great guy. Trust me, you'll love him."

"No, I won't. Because I'm not going to meet him. This is why I didn't tell you that my engagement was off. I didn't want you to feel sorry for me and then try to fix it. I don't need to be fixed."

Carla sat back. She was quiet for a moment, as though digesting this latest problem. "There has to be something I can do."

"Just be my friend."

"But I hate the thought of you being so miserable."

"I'm not."

"You're not?"

Gianna thought about it for a moment and then quite honestly said, "No, I'm not."

At least not yet. But when the day came, and it would very quickly, when she parted ways with Dario and Tito, she would miss them both dearly. But that was then and this was now.

"I just need you to keep this to yourself for a little longer. We're going to tell our families after the party. We don't want to cause any drama before the big event."

"I won't say a word. Because it might just give

you both time to realize what you have is real. It might not have started that way, but every time you talk about him, you light up. You're in love with him. And it appears you're the last one to know."

Gianna shook her head, chasing away her cousin's words. She refused to accept them. Because if Carla was right, then she'd just set herself up to be hurt again.

Was that a frown?

Dario drew closer to Gianna as she stood in front of a full-length mirror in their suite of rooms at his grandparent's villa. Oh, yes, that was most definitely a frown.

He stepped up behind her as she held up a satin hanger holding a white dress with bright flowers splashed across the material.

"Is that the dress you got this afternoon with your cousin?"

"It's one of them."

"I like it, but you don't seem to like it."

Gianna sighed as she lowered the dress. "It's not the clothes." When she turned quickly, her side brushed against him. He instinctively reached out to her, to keep her from losing her balance. When her gaze met his, there was attraction in her eyes. "It…it's this. It's us. Everyone thinks we're something we're not." Then she pointed to the bed where Tito was lying. "What are we going to do about tonight?"

"I was thinking eventually we'd sleep." He knew what she meant, but he wasn't so sure why she was blowing this development out of proportion.

She frowned at him. "And where will I sleep?"

"I figured next to me—"

She lightly slapped his arm. "Dario, get serious."

"I am. Why are you acting like it's our first time sharing a bed?"

Color bloomed in her cheeks. "Because this is different."

"It doesn't have to be."

Her gaze searched his. "What are you saying?"

"Do you want our relationship to be real?"

Her eyes widened. And then, as though realizing he was still touching her, she stepped back. "That wasn't our agreement."

"Forget our agreement. I shouldn't have suggested it in the first place. What do you want when this weekend is over?"

She shook her head. "You don't know what you're asking."

"Then explain it to me."

"I'm a disaster when it comes to relationships."

"Gianna, that's not true. It takes two to start a relationship and it takes two to end one."

"Not always. I let myself get ahead of things.

I set high expectations—too high for anyone to meet."

He sighed. "You haven't done that with me."

"Haven't I?" She gazed deeply into his eyes. "I've been pushing you to finish your book."

"And I have done that. After tomorrow night, I plan to tell my family that I'm walking away from the family business once and for all. It's all my brother's from now on."

"Are you doing that because it's what you really want? Or are you doing it because I talked you into it?"

"You didn't talk me into anything." Where was she getting this stuff from? And why wasn't she hearing him?

"I did. I push for what I think is the right thing whether it's for me or someone I care about. I just keep pushing and pushing."

Wait. Did she just say that she cared about him? It certainly sounded like it. He smiled.

It was at that moment that Gianna turned around. "What are you smiling about? Everything is a disaster."

"Everything is good. Really good." Maybe she just needed a moment to calm down. "I'll meet you downstairs. I need to take Tito for a walk."

Gianna nodded as she turned back to the mirror. She picked up a soft pink dress. It was simple yet elegant. But it worked for Gianna because she didn't need a dress to make a statement. She could do that all by herself.

As he walked away, he was certain that whatever dress she chose for the evening would be just fine. And he hoped her case of nerves would subside. He didn't want to leave her alone at this moment but he couldn't risk Tito having an accident. His grandmother was already unhappy about having a big dog in her house.

Later Dario had a surprise for Gianna. He was returning to Gemma. He hoped when she heard his news that it would put her worries to rest. Because he was anxious to see just where a real relationship would lead them.

CHAPTER SEVENTEEN

IT WAS QUITE a crowd.

All friends and acquaintances of Dario's family.

Gianna's stomach shivered with nerves. She shouldn't be here. She shouldn't be pretending she was something she wasn't.

She glanced down at her white flowery dress and hoped it looked all right. Carla and the saleswoman at the boutique had assured her that it was just perfect on her. Still, she wrung her hands together.

She continued to gaze down from the second-floor balcony, taking in all the smartly dressed people that had arrived for the party. In the living room, someone was playing the grand piano. It was an upbeat tune. She'd overheard that later in the evening there would be a famous singer. The name escaped her but it should be quite a show.

Just then Sergio and Vera Cappellini passed through the open front doors. A big smile lifted Gianna's lips. Her parents had really shown up.

She'd told them they didn't need to bother, but they'd insisted it would be rude not to attend and they were very interested in meeting Dario.

Gianna rushed down the stairs to greet them. But trying to move through the throng of people in the foyer was harder to do than she'd ever imagined. It took a lot of "Excuse me..." and "Pardon me..." until she reached them.

"Hi." She smiled and then hugged each of them. "It's so good to see you both."

"You look stunning." Her mother wore a mauve dress that Gianna recalled seeing her wear for one of her cousin's weddings. "I hope this is dressy enough. I don't want to embarrass you."

"Mamma, you look beautiful." And she meant it.

"Thank you, sweetie." Her mother beamed.

"See," her father said, "I told you the same thing and you didn't believe me."

Her mother looked lovingly at her father. "That's because you always say it, even when I'm in my pajamas with my hair going every which way."

He smiled at her. "That's because it's when you look the cutest." He leaned over and gave her mother a quick kiss. "I love you."

"I love you too."

Gianna loudly cleared her throat. "Should I leave you two lovebirds alone?"

"Of course not," her mother said. "You should know by now that your father is a flirt."

"Only with you," he corrected.

"I have some exciting news." Gianna told her parents about winning the competition.

After a bunch of congratulations and another round of hugs, her mother said, "Now where is the ring?"

Gianna lifted her hand to show her mother the glittery ring. Guilt settled on her. She needed to explain to her parents about her relationship with Dario, but with people bumping into them as they moved around the crowded room, there was no privacy.

"Wow!" Her mother took her hand to have a closer look. "That's a huge stone."

Heat filled Gianna's cheeks. She didn't deserve the ring. It wasn't like Dario was really going to marry her. Although things had changed after they'd slept together, had they changed that much? They hadn't finished their conversation. What did Dario want?

"Congratulations, honey." Her mother hugged her again. Then she turned to Gianna's father. "Go ahead. Congratulate your daughter."

Gianna knew this was hard on her father. She'd always been a daddy's girl. "It's okay."

"No, it isn't," her father said. He hugged her. "He better be a really great guy and treat you right or he has to deal with me."

When they pulled apart, Gianna said with utter honesty, "He's a great guy. And I'm positive you'll like him." She stood up on her tiptoes and looked around for Dario. And then she spotted him heading directly for her. She immediately smiled. "Here he comes."

When Dario finally made it to their little group, introductions were made. The men shook hands. She could tell her father was holding out on making his judgement until he knew Dario better, but her mother immediately enveloped Dario in a big hug.

This first meeting had gone so well that Gianna wished it were the real thing. Dario was the first man in her life that her parents had really taken to. What were they going to think when she told them the truth?

"We have to talk later," she said to her mother.

"Is something wrong?"

"No. It's just that I haven't seen you in a while and we need to catch up."

Her mother smiled. "You've got it, but it looks like you're needed elsewhere. Don't worry. We'll be fine on our own."

Gianna walked with Dario around the room, meeting guests. Other than their immediate families, she knew no one at this party. And there were so many names being bandied about that she couldn't remember any of them. So she smiled and made light conversation, avoiding using names at all costs.

Was this what it'd be like to be Dario's fiancée? Would she be expected to host parties? Would she have time to be the fiancée he needed and still pursue her own career? Or would she do what she always did and sacrifice what was important to her to make Dario happy?

Tonight was the night.

After all the guests had left, Dario intended to come clean to his family about his relationship with Gianna. He was done making excuses to put it off. And after all that, he would tell Gianna about his growing feelings for her.

He couldn't believe how much she'd changed his life in just a few very special weeks. She had worked her magic not only with his book but also with him. She showed him that love didn't have to hurt. It could be a good thing—a great thing. And he had no idea how to thank her—

"There you are, dear." His mother walked up to him with a big smile painted on her face. Her hand, with a giant rock on it, clutched the arm of an older gentleman. By the looks of the man, he was about his grandfather's age.

"Mother," Dario said in greeting. He didn't have much to say to her. Their relationship was about as distant as one could have and still refer to it as a relationship. "I didn't know you were invited."

She gave a short little laugh. "Why, of course, darling. After all, I am still family."

Dario coughed over that one. He made a point of sipping his drink as though to clear his throat. She wasn't family. Maybe she had been when he was born, but not for most of his life. And that choice had been hers—all hers.

"Where's Roger?" Dario asked about her third husband.

She frowned at him. "You mean Robert?"

Roger? Robert? It was close. It wasn't like he'd met the man more than once in passing. "Yes, him."

"We're no longer together," she said softly. "Fernando and I got married last month."

So she was on to husband number four. Dario didn't really care. He'd given up caring about what she did years ago. Still, he shook hands with the man.

One parent down, one to go. He craned his neck, checking the busy room for his father, but didn't see him anywhere. Dario didn't like to be caught off guard.

"If you're looking for your father, he couldn't make it. Last I heard, he was hiking up some mountain or some such thing."

Dario didn't know which shocked him more,

that his mother knew his father's whereabouts or that his father had taken up hiking.

"Oh, there you are." Gianna joined him. "Your grandmother sent me to find you."

He noticed his mother eyeing up Gianna. She wanted an introduction, but he didn't intend to give her one. It wasn't like she was truly his mother—a mother that cared about him—a mother who was involved in his life.

He was about to excuse himself and walk away when his mother said, "And who would you be?"

Gianna smiled. "I'm Dario's fiancée."

His mother's heavily painted eyes widened. She turned to him. "You're getting married?"

She said it so loud that all the people around him turned. Dario inwardly groaned. Now not only his family but also all their friends knew about the engagement. And the longer he was around his mother, the more he remembered why he didn't want to get engaged or married for that matter.

But it was too late to undo it now. People started to approach both him and Gianna. They shook their hands, asked for the wedding date, of which they had no answer, and then wished them well.

When there was a break in well-wishers, Dario turned to Gianna. "I'm so sorry about this."

"Me too. I never should have said anything to that woman about us being engaged."

"That was my mother."

Gianna's lips formed an O. Her eyes were full of questions, none of which she vocalized.

He leaned in close to her and said softly, "We'll tell our families after the party. They can get the word out to their friends."

"Sir." One of the wait staff approached them. "There's a gentleman here to see you."

Dario was confused. "Is he one of the guests?"

"No sir. He's waiting in the foyer." The waiter walked away.

Gianna looked at him. "Who do you think it is?"

He shrugged. "I'm not expecting anyone special. Let's go see."

He wasn't going to leave her in the living room to greet all these well-meaning guests on her own. Taking her hand in his, he headed for the door. He wasn't the only one. Both of his grandparents were headed that way. What was going on?

When he stepped into the foyer, his gaze connected with his agent, Ronaldo. What was he doing here?

His grandparents approached Dario. His grandfather asked, "Do you know this person?"

"Uh…yes, I do."

Ronaldo rushed over to him. "I'm so sorry to interrupt but this is just too big to text or say over the phone."

For a moment, Dario forgot they had an audience. "What did they say?"

"They loved the book. They thought the addition of the love story was brilliant. And the fact they are enemies ratcheted up the tension. We have a meeting with them next week to finalize the contract. Congratulations." They shook hands.

"Thank you." Dario turned to Gianna. "This is all thanks to you. I don't know how I'll ever thank you but I'll think of a way."

"What's going on?" his grandfather's sharp voice cut through Dario's excited haze. "What's this about a book?"

His grandmother elbowed his grandfather. "Quiet down and maybe he'll tell us."

Dario glanced around to see that they were not alone. His brother had finally arrived and was wearing a frown on his face. His mother had a similar expression. Her latest husband, Dario had already forgotten his name, looked utterly confused. Carla was also there. She smiled brightly at him. At least someone was happy for him.

He glanced over at Gianna. Her smile filled him with a calming warmth that started on the inside and worked its way out. The time had come to fill his family in on his secret.

CHAPTER EIGHTEEN

She was so happy for him.

Gianna couldn't stop smiling. And as she glanced around at his family, she couldn't understand why they weren't also happy for him. He'd worked so hard for this moment. But they didn't know that part yet.

When he sent her a hesitant look, she nodded at him to go ahead and tell everyone how his dream had come true.

She wanted to shrink away to the back of the crowd. After all, this was Dario's big moment, not hers. But as she started to walk away, he reached out for her hand and drew her back to his side. If he could face his family and reveal his amazing secret, she could stand there and be his biggest supporter.

"We're waiting," Franco called out.

Dario cleaned his throat. "I've been living what I'd guess you'd call a double life."

"A what?" his grandmother asked.

"For the past two years, I've been spending my

days at the office but my evenings and weekends I've spent writing."

Gianna smiled and nodded as though to attest to all his hard work. Still none of his family smiled.

"Oh," his grandmother said, "you have a hobby. That's nice, dear. Everyone needs one of those."

"Not a hobby, Nonna. It's my career."

His grandfather muttered something under his breath and shook his head.

Franco spoke up. "You surely don't think you can make it writing one book? Who's going to buy it? You're a nobody."

That was when his agent spoke up. "He's not a nobody. He's D.J. March."

This drew everyone's attention. Franco's face scrunched up in confusion. "You're trying to tell us you're a famous author?"

"He is," Gianna spoke up, hoping to stir up some excitement in his family. "It's how we met." Oops. She wasn't supposed to say that. She was so excited that the words slipped past her lips unchecked.

"Why didn't you tell us?" his grandmother asked.

"Because… I wasn't sure what I wanted to do with my life." Dario turned his gaze to Gianna. "Well, that's not quite true. I wasn't sure I had what it takes to make writing a lifelong career."

His grandmother looked at him with caring eyes. "And now you know that it's what you want to do?"

"It is. Gianna helped me figure it out."

"Ah, this is a waste of time," his grandfather spat out.

"I agree," Dario's mother said. "The family business is worth a fortune. Why would you walk away from it?"

Gianna wanted to answer this for him. She couldn't believe his family was treating him this way. But she knew Dario had to do this on his own.

Dario cleared his throat. "I'm walking away because Franco is the rightful heir to the family business. He's the oldest and he has worked the hardest to see that it flourishes. My heart just isn't in it, not like his."

The two brothers' gazes connected for just a moment and she sensed some sort of understanding had silently flowed between them. Franco looked relieved.

His grandfather stepped forward. "So you're just going to sit around writing books for the rest of your life?"

Dario shrugged. "If I'm lucky enough."

Ronaldo moved next to Dario. "Trust me. Dario has a bright future ahead of him. I didn't get a chance to tell you the best part. There's a bidding war for the movie rights to your first book."

Dario didn't say a word for a moment. Gianna couldn't blame him. It was a lot to take in. They were making a movie based on his book. His characters would be brought to life for all the world to see. She was so proud of him.

"That's amazing."

Dario smiled.

"Pretty cool, huh?" Ronaldo grinned. "We've got to get you packed and on the road. The publisher wants you attending book signings and conferences promoting the first book. They really want a big build up for the release of book two. And then they'll want your input with the script for the movie, so plan on a trip to Hollywood."

Gianna grew quiet as she listened to how Dario's world was about to change. She was so very happy for him, but as reality settled in, she was sad for herself. Because after years of living out of a suitcase, she was ready to settle down in Gemma and sleep in her own comfy bed each night.

And then there was Dario. His career was just taking off and he would be on the go. Here, there and everywhere. His fans would want to meet him, take pictures with him and her gut told her that his second book would be an even a bigger hit than the first. And she wouldn't do anything to hold him back.

Franco stepped forward. "So this is what you've been working on while you were at Lake Como?"

Dario nodded. "Yes, and to buy myself the time I needed away from the business to write, I let you all believe that we're engaged. But that's not true."

"What?" It was a collective shocked response.

"You mean you're not getting married?" his grandmother's gaze narrowed as it moved between the two of them.

Gianna remained silent. This was not the way she would have handled it. And it was then that she noticed her parents had joined the group. Her mother looked devastated and her father looked angry. She felt awful.

"No." Dario shook his head. "We're not. It was all a charade."

Those words were like an arrow to her heart. He seemed to dismiss everything they'd shared these past few weeks as nothing important. Now that all his dreams were coming true, she felt dismissed, like yesterday's news.

"I'm sorry for that," Dario said. "We never planned on it working out this way. One thing led to another and then one person knew, then two people knew and then it all got out of hand."

"So it's all over?" her father asked. "The ring was just for show?"

"The ring is a gift." Dario glanced at her but Gianna couldn't quite meet his gaze. "I hope Gianna will keep it."

She couldn't listen to this anymore. Dario was acting like they were strangers—mere acquaintances. And it was then that she realized she'd fallen in love with him. She was such a fool. He was her third and final fiancé. She was done with romance.

She turned and started toward the front door. She was leaving, even if she had to walk. She just couldn't stand here and listen to Dario talk about them like they'd never shared any of those special moments. Maybe the engagement was fake but she didn't think the rest of it had been.

She could hear her father continuing to drill Dario with questions. Good. It would give her time to get away. She disappeared into the crowd as it appeared everyone had moved from the living room to the foyer to find out what was going on.

She kept her head down as she slowly made it to the door. At last, she stepped out into the evening air. For the first time since Dario told the world they were fakes, she could breath. But her eyes stung with unshed tears. She blinked them away. She couldn't cry for a relationship that had never existed—because it had clearly never been real in Dario's mind or heart.

She kept walking. She didn't have a destination in mind. She supposed that eventually she'd have to return to the grand villa as her things were still there, but not yet.

"Gianna! Wait."

She knew that voice. It was Dario. What was he doing out here? Why was he following her?

She kept walking at the same pace. She wasn't going to stop. She didn't want to talk to him. There was nothing left to say—he'd said it all.

"Gianna?" He reached out, touching her upper arm. "Didn't you hear me?"

"I just needed some air."

"Can you stop so we can talk?"

"I don't think there's anything left to say."

He stepped in front of her, blocking her way. "Gianna, what's the matter? I thought we agreed that we were going to tell everyone the truth. I mean, I know it wasn't exactly the right time, but it just all came out."

She averted her gaze. She didn't want him to read her emotions. "It's fine. Everything is fine."

"If everything is fine, you wouldn't be out here. Alone. Talk to me."

"I don't have anything to say." And then she realized she never got a chance to congratulate him on his big accomplishment. This time, she lifted her gaze to meet his. "Congratulations on your book sale and movie deal. I knew you could do it."

"Thank you. But I know that's not what has you upset."

"Why do you keep saying that I'm upset? I'm fine. Everything is out in the open and now we can get on with our lives."

"What if I said that I didn't want to get on with my life, not without you?"

Her heart skipped a beat. What was he saying?

In the next heartbeat, she realized that no matter what he said, they weren't destined to be together. He had to go off and chase his dream. She couldn't hold him back—no matter how much it hurt her. He deserved to ride his rising star as far as it'd take him.

And she'd finally figured out what made her truly happy—her photography. She was done reinventing herself to fit into a man's life. She had to follow her own dream.

"Stop," she said. And then she did the one thing she knew she had to do to end things once and for all. "We got caught up in an act, but it's over now. You have a big publishing career to enjoy and another book to write because I can't get enough of Lavar and Ator." Then she slipped the ring from her finger. She placed it in his hand and wrapped his fingers around it. "Take it."

"But it's yours."

She shook her head. Her heart felt as though

it were cracking in two. "It's best we end things here. I have to go."

She turned back toward his grandparents' villa. She had to get her things and go. Being around Dario was too painful. She was going to miss him for a long, long time. But she took solace in knowing he'd be happy.

CHAPTER NINETEEN

HOME AGAIN.

Gianna didn't smile.

Today, life felt as though it were playing a bit of déjà vu with her. The last time she'd returned from a trip, she'd thought she was at her lowest point. It had been the end of another relationship and the end of a prestigious job. This time, she'd returned the winner of a prestigious competition and her relationship hadn't actually ended because it'd never really existed. However, she felt so much lower.

The truth was she'd lost the man she loved.

Even thought she'd done the walking, it didn't hurt any less. Tears welled up in her eyes. She blinked them back. She refused to dissolve into a fit of tears. Again. This was for the best—for both them. But at the moment, it sure didn't feel like it.

One day faded into two. Dario called every day and left messages for her to call him. She deleted those messages before she caved into her desire to phone him just to hear his voice again. She knew it would just make matters worse.

Knock-knock.

She wasn't expecting anyone. Maybe if she just sat there quietly, they'd go away. Because there was absolutely no one she wanted to talk to—

"Gianna! I know you're in there." Carla's voice echoed through the door. "I'm coming in."

The door creaked open. Gianna admonished herself for never locking the door. But this was Gemma where crime just didn't happen.

Carla stepped into the living room. Worry showed in her eyes. "I've been trying to call you." She rushed over and sat down on the couch next to her. "Are you all right?"

"I'm fine." Her wavering voice said she was anything but.

"Why did you leave so suddenly?"

"Once the truth about the engagement was out, I was no longer needed."

"Dario looked devastated after you left. He quickly disappeared."

Gianna met her cousin's gaze. "You know we were never really a couple."

"The only people that believe that are you and Dario. Everyone else could see what you two couldn't or wouldn't accept—that you're crazy in love with each other. Otherwise, why would you be sitting in here with the blinds drawn, staring blindly at the television?" Carla focused on the television. "What are you watching?"

"I have no idea." She hadn't even realized the television was still on. Gianna grabbed the remote and turned it off.

Gianna needed to talk to someone—to have Carla understand her actions—to convince herself that she'd done the right thing. "I can't hold him back. It wouldn't be fair. And in the end, I think he'd come to resent me. And I just couldn't stand for that to happen."

"Maybe it doesn't have to be either-or. Maybe there's a compromise."

"It won't work. I'd rather think of what might have been if the timing had been different."

"Are you sure you want to settle for what-if instead of what-is?"

Did her cousin have a point? Was she just hiding behind excuses of why they couldn't be together because she was afraid that if she really gave them a chance—if she admitted her feelings for Dario—that she'd get hurt again? Was he worth taking that big leap of faith?

He didn't want to be here.

He didn't want to be around people—unless their name was Gianna Cappellini.

And yet his brother had shown up at his apartment door and insisted he go with him to Sunday dinner at their grandparents. He said his grandfather had a big announcement and they both had to be there. And Franco wasn't leaving without him.

Reluctantly, Dario had taken a quick shower and put on a fresh suit because his grandparents insisted on dressing for dinner. Tito whined about being left behind, but he knew how his grandmother felt about having the dog in the house. It was better this way and he certainly didn't expect to be gone long.

When they arrived, his grandmother insisted that business wait until after dinner. Dario was so caught up in his own troubles that he didn't think too much about what his grandfather had to say. All Dario could think about was Gianna's retreating back as she left him—saying they didn't belong together. How could she say that?

They got along great. She made him smile and he thought he did the same for her. She made him reach for his dreams, no matter how hard it had been for him. She opened his eyes to love and that it didn't always have to be disastrous like his parents or cold and distant like his grandparents.

Love could be fun. It could be warm. And it could be fiery. But most of all, it meant spending time with your best friend—the person you could talk to about anything. At least he'd thought Gianna had become his best friend. Had he only been seeing what he'd wanted to see?

And then there was Tito, who had barely eaten

since Gianna's departure. Even his dog was down in the dumps without her around. How did you explain to a pup that the woman he loved to follow around and beg treats from would no longer be a part of his life? Dario didn't have the words because he didn't know how to explain it to himself. One moment, things were fine, and in the next moment, it was over. She was gone.

"Dario?" His brother waved at him. "Nonna was speaking to you."

Dario blinked and turned to his grandmother. "Sorry. What did you say?"

"You haven't eaten. Are you feeling all right?"

He glanced down at his plate, finding that he'd moved the food around but he hadn't eaten a thing. He had absolutely no appetite.

He glanced around at the other plates, finding they'd finished eating. Good. It was almost time for him to leave. Just a little bit longer.

"Now that dinner is over," his grandfather began, "Dario, I know you were excited the other night and you said things you didn't mean—"

"I meant everything I said. I quit." Dario had been expecting some pushback from his grandfather. "I'm not turning my back on the business. And if there comes a time when I'm needed to step in, I'll do it. But for now, Franco can run the business. He's good at it and he likes it."

"And what?" his grandfather said. "You're going to just write books?"

"Yes." And he wasn't going to feel guilty about his choice. It was right for him. And it was right for Franco to have control of the company.

"This is about that woman." His grandfather frowned. "She talked you into quitting."

Dario's body tensed. How dare his grandfather blame any of this on Gianna. It took all his self-restraint to keep his voice calm and level. "Her name is Gianna. She is the kindest, most thoughtful woman. And she didn't talk me into anything. She helped me see what makes me the happiest."

His grandfather sighed as he leaned back in his chair. "Well, when things don't work out the way you planned, just remember that I warned you."

Dario shoulders tensed. It was time to go before he said something he'd regret. He pushed his chair back from the table and then stood. "I have to go."

"I didn't make my announcement," his grandfather said. "It might change your mind about walking away from the business."

His gaze connected with his brother's, who nodded for him to sit down. Dario subdued a groan of frustration and sat once more. As soon as his grandfather had his say, he was out of there.

His grandfather leaned forward, resting his elbows on the table. "I've been going over the books with the accountants. And I know you two were anxious to expand the line of products, but the online sales just aren't enough to sustain the extra products. I'm afraid we'll have to cut them back."

Dario's gaze moved to his brother, seeing how his face had creased with a frown. This is what they'd been worried about. It's what they'd been working to stop from happening, but seeing as their grandfather hadn't signed over full control to them, he still had the final say.

"At least give Franco more time to line up some stores or restaurants to carry the lines," Dario said, hating the thought of all their hard work of finding the right spices and organic herbs just going to waste. They both believed in the products. And so would the consumers as soon as they tried them. But to do that, they had to be readily for sale.

His grandfather turned on him. His brows were drawn together in a firm line. "Why would you care? Remember, you quit."

"It doesn't mean I don't care about the future of the company. Franco and I have worked hard to bring back some of the past products."

His grandfather stood. "You have no say."

"But I do." Franco also stood. "You can't do this. I'm working on getting bigger exposure for our lesser-known products."

Their grandfather crossed his arms. "It'd have to be a very good plan—"

"It is. I'm going to get them back in the Falco Ristorantes—"

"You can't do that!"

"Wait and see." Franco's gaze challenged their grandfather.

"You...you can't. That man's nothing but a cheat. I refuse to do business with him."

"Who?" Both brothers spoke at once.

"Carlo Falco is not to be trusted." Their grandfather's face was red with anger.

Dario couldn't remember the last time his grandfather got this worked up. What was Nonno talking about? And why was this the first time he was hearing about Carlo Falco being disreputable?

"Giuseppe, I can't believe you."

Everyone's attention turned to Nonna. Her narrowed gaze was laser focused on her husband. The tension in the room was so charged that it practically crackled.

"You don't understand—"

"I understand just fine," their grandmother said. "You've been gambling again. And after you swore to me that you were done playing cards—"

"But I did quit. This was a long time ago. If you don't believe me, just ask the boys how long ago our products were removed from the Falco restaurants."

Both Dario and Franco assured their grandmother that it'd been years since the deal with the Falco's had fallen through. But they'd both been under the impression that it'd been a business decision—not a personal one. *Nonno was a gambler? Wow!* Dario wondered what else he didn't know about his grandparents.

Their grandfather's gaze moved to Franco. "You have six months to increase the profit margin, otherwise I'm stepping back in as acting president and I will make any changes necessary."

The men glared at each other. Tensions had never been this high in the family. And though Dario felt bad for his brother, he was glad he was out of it. His grandfather's constant interference was just too much.

"Enough!" their grandmother said. "I won't stand for anymore of this. Now sit. Dessert will be here shortly."

Dario glanced down at the table, finding the dinner dishes had been cleared from the table during the argument. Dario turned to his grandmother. "I'm going to go."

"Please don't go so soon," she said. "We see you so rarely."

"Let him go," his grandfather said. "He didn't even touch his dinner."

"That's because he's in love." Nonna sent Dario a sympathetic smile. "You should go to Gianna and work things out."

Dario shook his head. "It won't do any good. She said we're over."

"She might have said it but I don't think she meant it. I saw the way she looked at you. She's a woman in love." Nonna's eyes widened as though she'd thought of something. "Stay here. I'll be right back."

Dario didn't want to stay, but he had a soft spot for his grandmother. She wasn't overly affectionate but he knew without a doubt that she loved him and his brother. While she was gone, fresh fruit and some gelato were served. His favorites. He took a bite but it didn't appeal to him.

Nonna quickly returned. "Here you go."

He accepted the small jeweler's box from her. "What is it?"

"It's something I've been holding for you for a very long time. Open it."

He did as she asked. Inside was a diamond ring. It was beautiful in a simplistic way.

"It belonged to your great-grandmother, my mother." She turned to Franco. "Don't worry. I have a ring saved for you too."

"I won't be needing it," Franco said firmly.

Their grandmother sent him a knowing smile. "Trust me. Love will find you when you least expect it." While Franco shook his head, Nonna turned her attention back to Dario. "I've been waiting until you found the right woman to give it to you. Gianna is the right one for you. I knew it as soon as I saw the two of you together."

He knew his grandmother was trying to help but this was just making it harder on him. He closed the box and slid it across the table toward her. "I can't take it."

"Sure you can."

"But I already gave Gianna a ring—a much larger ring—and she rejected it and me."

"Maybe it wasn't the right ring with the right proposal."

Was that it? His grandmother was a wise woman. But could a diamond ring—this family heirloom—change her mind? He honestly didn't know.

"And there's one more thing," his grandmother said. She moved to the doorway and then reached into the hallway. "The maid found this under your bed when they were cleaning your old room. I thought it might be important."

When she held out a large rectangular-shaped package covered with heavy brown wrapping paper, he realized it was the same kind he'd noticed in Gianna's office. And then he saw his name scrolled across the front in Gianna's very distinctive handwriting.

He ripped off the paper, finding one of her prints inside with a note taped to it.

This should be the winning photo.
Too bad there wasn't a category to enter it.
But it is the photo from my heart.
Love, Gianna

"What is it?" his grandmother asked.

"Yes, show us," his brother said.

"Just wait." Dario removed the taped note from the front of the picture.

He gazed at the silhouette of him and Tito walking down a shady wooded path. His back was to the camera, which was the reason he couldn't remember her taking this photo, and he was glancing down at Tito at the same time Tito was glancing up at him. In the background, there was a break in the trees where the sunshine gleamed down. It was a very striking photo. He absolutely loved it.

And it appeared just as he needed a sign. He knew what to do now—follow his heart—straight back to Gemma. There was a woman there that he was madly in love with. Now he just needed to convince her that they belonged together.

CHAPTER TWENTY

THIS JUST HAD to work.

Dario had spent all of Sunday evening staring at the modest diamond ring his grandmother had given him. If a big splashy ring wouldn't sway Gianna's decision, would a smaller ring make any difference?

And then he'd recalled his grandmother's words about the right ring with the right proposal. It was true that he'd never really proposed. Not exactly.

He remembered how marriage had ended with his parents. They not only got rid of each other but also their children. He'd be lying if he didn't fear the same thing might happen to him.

Perhaps that's why he'd skirted around the subject of marriage—why he hadn't laid his heart on the line. The thought of being rejected once more by someone he loved was devastating.

But now that he'd officially stepped away from the family business, he knew his fictional characters wouldn't be enough company. No one, real or fictional, could replace Gianna.

He thought of Ator and how he'd risked his realm in order to be with Sefinna—the enemy. If he could write about people taking big risks for love, why couldn't he do the same thing?

First thing Monday morning, he started to put his plan in motion. He was going to show Gianna that they belonged together. Because they were stronger together—they were happier together— they were their best together. He believed that with all his heart.

By Wednesday, his plan was in full motion. He had enlisted a little help from Carla. If anyone knew Gianna's likes and dislikes, it was her cousin. He hadn't filled her in on his whole plan though, just a piece of it.

At noon on Wednesday, he parked his car in Gemma. Tito was anxious to get out and stretch his legs and so Dario decided to walk the rest of the way to Gianna's villa. He just hoped she was home.

Tito knew the way and the closer they got to the villa, the faster the dog moved. And then when the villa came into sight, Tito took off at a run with his tail swishing back and forth. This was the happiest he'd seen his dog in days. It appeared he wasn't the only one who had missed her.

"Tito! Come back. Tito."

The dog didn't slow down.

Well, this wasn't exactly how he'd envisioned their meeting, but then again, maybe Tito would soften her up for him. After all, not even Gianna could deny her fondness for his dog.

Woof! Woof-woof!

Tito raced up to the closed door that was normally open. Dario now worried that she really wasn't home and he'd have to wait even longer to speak to her. *Please say it isn't so.* He willed her to be home.

Tito jumped at the door as he continued barking and putting up such a fuss that no one could miss it. If Gianna was home, she would open the door.

And she did.

Dario's heart soared at the sight of her. He stopped walking and merely took in her beauty. It felt like a lifetime since he'd last seen her. Oh, how he'd missed her.

Tito's tail moved in a blur. He jumped up, his front paws landing on her chest as he leaned in and licked Gianna's cheek. Gianna hugged him and fussed over him, making Dario jealous that he couldn't switch places with his dog.

Go, Tito! He smiled at his silly dog.

And then her gaze swung around, searching for him. When she spotted him, the smile faded from her face. Oh, no. That wasn't good at all.

He started walking again. Much faster this time. He didn't want to give her a chance to slip away behind a closed door. To his relief, she stayed where she was and continued to fuss over Tito, who ate up every sweet, crooning word she sent his way.

"What are you doing here?" Gianna asked as she straightened.

"Technically, I can still be here." He'd use any excuse to speak to her. "Remember our rental agreement?"

She crossed her arms. "And did you forget it ends today?"

"True enough." Not exactly the greeting he'd hoped for, but she hadn't slammed the door in his face so he'd take it. It took him a moment to re-member his excuse to come see her. He reached for the box under his arm. "I promised you this."

Her puzzled gaze moved to the box. "What is it?"

"Here, take it."

She was hesitant but eventually took it from him. She untied the twine from the white box and then lifted the lid. "Your book."

"I told you that once it was sold, you'd be the first one to read it."

"I…uh, thank you. But you didn't have to bring it all this way."

"Actually, I did. I have something I want you to see." He hadn't even gotten all the words out be-fore she started to shake her head. "Please come with me."

"Dario, it's not a good idea. It's best just to leave things as is."

"I disagree."

She frowned. "We've been through all this and it's been decided."

"No. You decided. I didn't. Just give me a few minutes of your time, and if you still want me to go, you won't have to see me again."

She sighed. "You aren't going to leave until I agree, are you?"

Woof-woof!

Gianna looked at Tito and smiled. "Figures you'd be on his side." She turned back to Dario. "Okay. Let's go." It was then that she got a puzzled look on her face. "Where's your car?"

"In the village. Tito wanted to stretch his legs. He doesn't get as much exercise now that we're back in the city."

She turned back to Tito. "You poor baby. You should make Dario walk you more."

When she turned to put the book in the house, Dario said, "Bring it."

Her fine brows scrunched together. "What for?"

"You'll see."

And then they started to walk toward the village. Dario knew he still had a shot with her, but he didn't let his hopes get too high. There was still a chance she didn't feel as deeply for him as he did her.

* * *

What was he up to?

Gianna wasn't so sure what made her decide to go with him. She didn't even know where they were headed, because as soon as they'd reached the village, they climbed in Dario's car and he started driving. Destination unknown. He was certainly acting very mysterious.

She told herself to stick to her decision for each of them to go their separate ways. But with each passing kilometer, her resolve weakened.

She chanced a glance his way. While his attention was on traffic, she took in his handsome face. Her heart beat faster. Her gaze zeroed in on his lips. She missed his kisses. Those kisses that weren't supposed to mean anything—that were supposed to be just for show—they meant everything to her. She would cherish them forever—

Dario turned in her direction. She jerked her attention to the road ahead. Her heart raced. Did he know she'd been staring at him? Heat swirled in her chest and rushed to her cheeks. Why exactly had she agreed to this little adventure?

As they entered Como, she let herself become distracted with the sights. Como was a city whereas Gemma was just a small village. They were very different in size and energy. Where Gemma was laidback, Como was lively.

Dario pulled to a stop in front of some small shops. Tourists with their hands full of shopping bags made their way along the walk. Gianna had absolutely no idea what they were doing here.

"Dario, what are you up to?"

He was currently attaching a leash to Tito's collar. "I'll show you." He and Tito rounded the front of the car and met her on the sidewalk. "Don't forget the book."

Was he serious? What did he plan, a book reading? Wasn't that usually only done with published books? She wasn't quite sure since she'd never attended a book reading. Still, she did as he asked.

When she straightened, he said, "Right this way."

They walked a short distance before coming to a stop in front of a vacant shop. Dario unlocked the door, stepped inside and flipped on the lights.

"What do you think?" he asked.

"Is this yours?" She was confused. It certainly didn't look like the type of place where he'd want to write his books.

"No." He turned to her. "This is yours, if you want it."

"What? I… I don't understand."

He smiled at her, making her stomach dip. "Maybe you should open the box in your arms and start to read."

Now she was really confused. He wanted her to read his book now? "I don't think we have time for me to read it now."

He continued to smile. "Trust me. Just start reading."

And so she opened the box. The book was printed out on white printer paper. The top sheet was the cover page with *The Clash of Lavar* by D.J. March. The next page was the copyright page. But it was the third page that harnessed her full attention. It was the dedication page.

To the most amazing woman I've ever known.
You've shown me that true love really
does exist.
I love you now and always.
Will you marry me?

Her mouth gaped as her heart pitter-pattered. Her gaze rose to meet his. He reached in his pocket and removed a black velvet ring box. He opened it and held it out to her as he knelt down on one knee.

"I'm sorry I let you walk away. It was a huge mistake. My life isn't the same without you in it."

Her eyes misted over with tears of joy. Was this really happening? She felt as though she were having an out-of-body experience.

"I love you, Gianna, with all my heart. And I know if we try, we can find a way to be together while we both chase our own dreams."

The happy tears spilled onto her cheeks as she pressed a shaky hand to her lips.

"Gianna Cappellini, will you do me the honor of being my wife?"

Every reason why they wouldn't work faded away. In his eyes, she found the courage to follow her heart. "Yes. Yes, I will."

He stood and slipped the ring on her finger. He gazed deep into her eyes as he swiped the tears from her cheeks. And then he pressed his lips to hers.

She didn't know how long they stood there in each other's arms. However long it was, it wasn't nearly long enough. When he pulled back, he lost his balance. She reached out to steady him.

It was then that they realized Tito had given them his blessing. He'd once again wrapped them up in his leash. They both smiled as they unwound themselves.

Gianna still had one more question. "I don't understand about this shop."

"It's my wedding gift to you. You've been talking about opening a gallery and I thought you'd like it."

"Like it? I love it." She glanced all around, imagining her prints on the walls. "But if I'm here and you're traveling the world promoting your book—"

"Trust me. We'll make it work. After all, we can hire help and I don't plan to do a lot of traveling. I'll have a beautiful wife to cherish." Tito barked, causing them to laugh. "And a pup to play with. Not to mention my next book to write."

"And I might go with you now and then. I can take pictures while you visit with your fans."

He laughed. "I'm telling you, I'm not famous. I'll be known as the husband of the famous photographer."

"As long as we're together, it'll all work out." And for the first time, she let herself believe it. Together, they could do anything.

EPILOGUE

Several weeks later,
Fiorire Botanical Gardens, Lake Como

RINGS WERE EXCHANGED.

And there wasn't a dry eye in the lush garden.

Okay. So maybe it was just Carla's eyes that were damp. She swiped at them. True love had won out over everything. She was so happy for her cousin and Dario.

That's the way it should always be—marrying for love. However, Carla's father was nagging her to settle down and marry. Her father wouldn't care if love was involved, so long as she married a man fit to run the family business. But she'd set him straight. If—a big if—she married, it'd be on her own timetable.

And that thought was like a bone that stuck in her throat. She'd given up striking out on her own when her mother had died. She'd focused on her education and delved into learning everything there was to know about Falco's Fresco

Ristorante. She had worked her way up through the company until she felt ready to stand in for her father, but he wouldn't hear of it.

She was supposed to have been born a boy. Finding out he had a daughter instead of the longed-for son had been a big blow for her father. Still, she'd been named after him, but nothing she did convinced him that she could be a strong, reliable heir—all because she was a female.

Even when he had his heart attack a couple of months ago, he'd argued with her but she'd done what needed to be done. She'd made the day-to-day decisions. She'd kept the business on track. And she'd closed a few big deals. Still, it wasn't enough for her father.

"You may kiss the bride." The minister's voice drew her back to the service.

"Aw…" Carla smothered her reaction.

And then Gianna turned to her, her eyes shimmering with happiness. She didn't have to say anything. The joy was written all over her face. And Carla couldn't be happier for her. If any two people deserved to get their happily-ever-after, they did.

Carla handed over the bouquet of purple lilies and white roses and Gianna turned back to her new husband, slipping her hand in the crook of his arm.

"Ladies and gentlemen, I'd like to introduce for the first time, Mr. and Mrs. Dario Marchello."

The string quartet started to play the recessional as the newlyweds made their way down the aisle. When they were halfway down, Carla's gaze moved to the best man.

When their gazes met, her heart picked up its pace as heat warmed her cheeks. What was wrong with her? It wasn't like she was into Franco. As she'd come to learn, he was just like her father—always thinking about business. The last thing she wanted to do was play second fiddle to a business. And she wasn't even looking for a man in her life right now—she had other priorities.

Still, as she slipped her hand in the crook of his strong arm, she had to admit that she didn't mind having him next to her. They paused for the camera and then continued down the aisle.

As they passed by her father, he glowered at her. She wondered what had elicited such a response from him. Was he still disgruntled that she'd used her own judgment over a matter at the office instead of doing as he'd demanded—even if her decision had saved the company both money and jobs? Or was it perhaps her escort that he didn't care for?

"I guess you're next," Franco said, drawing her from her thoughts.

"Next?"

"You know, getting married."

Once they were out of the way of the next couple, she turned to him. "I'm not sure what you're getting at but I have no plans to get married anytime soon."

"Really?" He arched a disbelieving brow.

What did he know that she didn't? Had there been some erroneous rumor in the paper? They were always making up headlines.

"What have you heard?"

"Your father was overheard saying you would be married by the end of the year."

"He what?" Her brain was still trying to process this bit of information. "Whoever said that is mistaken."

Franco shook his head. "I don't think so. I overheard him myself and he was very matter-of-fact."

She pressed her lips firmly together, holding back her heated words. Her father had been difficult with his need to dictate her life even before his heart attack, but since his recovery, he was utterly impossible. And this explained the solid string of business dinners that he'd insisted she accompany him to—always with an unattached businessman within her age range.

She frowned. "He shouldn't have said that."

Franco held up his hands innocently. "Don't kill the messenger. I thought you knew what he was up to."

She sighed. Franco was right. He had nothing to do with her father and his misguided plans. She knew the heart attack had shaken him up, but this was going too far. "I should have known, but I've been distracted lately with his failing health—something he doesn't worry enough about."

"I'm sure he's just worried about you, about what will happen to you if something happens to him. How is he doing?"

She resisted the urge to shrug. "According to him, he's just fine. According to everyone else, including his doctors, he needs to slow down."

"I'm sorry to hear that. So you're running the business now?"

She nodded. "For now, I am." She caught sight of the bride. "I really need to go."

"Maybe later we could talk a little business."

"Uh…maybe. Now's not really the time." She pasted on a big smile as she moved toward her cousin. "You make the most beautiful bride."

"Thank you. Maybe you'll be next." Gianna waggled her fine brows as she teased her.

"Don't you start too. It appears my father is intent on finding me a husband."

"Really?" When Carla nodded, Gianna continued. "He told you this?"

"Worse. Franco just informed me."

"He wants you to marry Franco—"

"Shh…" Heat rushed up Carla's neck and set her cheeks aflame. "Don't let anyone hear you say that, especially your new husband."

"Well? Does he?"

"No," she said quickly, putting an end to that thought. At least she didn't think her father would have such a preposterous thought in mind. Would he?

Her father could be quite manipulative when he wanted to be. She just needed to outsmart him and show him that she was fine on her own. She didn't need him or anyone arranging her marriage. She refused to be told what she should and shouldn't do.

These weren't the olden days where a woman needed a man. She would do fine on her own, both in business and personally. But first, she had to find a way to convince her father that he could trust her with his beloved company.

* * * * *

Look out for the next story in the
Wedding Bells at Lake Como duet
Coming soon!

And if you enjoyed this story,
check out these other great reads from
Jennifer Faye

Fairytale Christmas with the Millionaire
The Italian's Unexpected Heir
The CEO, the Puppy and Me

All available now!